MourneQuest
The Devil's Coachroad

For Sandra, Frank and Micheal

MourneQuest
The Devil's Coachroad

Garry McElherron

Illustrations by John Farrelly
And Alan Perry

O:cellaris

First published 2016

www.mournequest.com

ISBN 978-1-326-76966-6

Contents

Chapter 1

The Wake

An angry wind swept through the deserted harbour of Springwell Port and the bells on the barnacled fishing boats clanged as though an invisible hand had suddenly rocked them. The seagulls and oystercatchers sleeping on the decks took flight into the thick swell of billowing clouds that loomed overhead drowning out the silver light of the full moon.

The same wind licked its way up the hillside, past the old mill and began to whip a black ribbon of a laurel wreath that hung on the half-door of Jack Turner's cottage. The lucky horseshoe was now hidden beneath this new black marker. The wreath told any passer-by that Death had been a recent visitor to this home.

Dim candles flickered behind the lace curtains and within the cottage, in her room, lay Nanna Tess, covered from head to foot in a sheet of snow-white linen, her eyes closed and her thin bony fingers intertwined with a single red rose. Jack's mother Martha had painted a glowing complexion on Tess' cheeks. In fact, his mother had made all the preparations for the wake; from covering every picture on the cottage walls with cloth to ensuring that the small mirror that sat on Nanna's bedside table remained overturned. It was an old Irish superstition that a mirror could capture the spirit of a dead person but Martha knew the Old Irish tradition well and she guaranteed no reflection would come near Tess.

For more than two days, Jack hardly left his Nanna Tess' side, in all that time he sat in the corner of the room and watched in silence at the comings and goings of the people who arrived to see his dead great grandmother. The men removed their cloth caps when they entered the wake room and the women bowed their veiled heads as their lips moved silently in prayer. The whole thing wasn't new to Jack and the last time there had been a wake in the house flashed through his mind. The thought of it made his face flush and a painful tingle ran through his fingers. He didn't want to remember his late brother right now. He wanted only to think of his Nanna Tess.

Jack had found Nanna Tess the day before when he had returned with his mother from the pier. They stood for hours waiting there for Jack's father Matthew but it was fruitless. The short journey back to the cottage had seemed endless and by the time he'd reached Nanna Tess' bedroom door a seething fire blazed in his stomach. He ran straight into her room and yelled at her that his father had not come back from his fishing trip as she had promised.

His anger quickly dissolved, replaced by utter despair. He stood in the middle of Tess' room and stared at a frail old woman, ashen white, blue-lipped and as dead as his own hopes and dreams. His heart ached in a way he thought only possible from his brother's and father's loss. Just as the first tear welled up in his eye, he smiled a little, because resting on Nanna Tess' forehead was the Obsidian Stone.

When Tess had given the stone to Jack on the cliff side in the InBetween, he knew she had used its magic to appear as a young fresh-faced girl in a red dress. When he first held the stone it had been as black as night but a thick line of white quartz glittered through its centre like the stars of the Milky Way. Jack also knew that after he had been brought back to life by the stone, the vein of quartz had become much thinner but now the shimmering quartz had vanished completely. The stone was now pure obsidian, and as his Nanna would say 'as black as the devil's heart.' The last piece of magic drained the stone completely and somehow Jack could sense it.

He carefully pocketed the stone and he would never let it out his possession ever again. It was now a link between him and his Nanna Tess. They had shared its magic.

Jack noticed the slight odour of dried rose petals that lingered in the bedroom. It reminded him of the smell that escaped from the old battered box Nanna Tess had given him. The box that contained his first dandelion, his first wish, and the ferocious pains that had boiled inside him on his return to the cottage were replaced by a wave of calm. Whatever Nanna Tess had done Jack knew that the magic she had used was very powerful. He took a closer look at her face, at her thin lips, and he saw a dimple in her cheek he'd never seen before. In death, he saw his Nanna Tess' true smile, faint though it was. He could see the tiny wrinkled lines in the corners of her eyes and he knew she must have been smiling when she died. It gave him great comfort for he knew she died happy and was now in a better place, a wondrous place, a place set aside for one of the last ElderFolk.

"Sorry for your loss Mrs Turner, and you too of course, my dear Master Jack," said a voice as dry as dust. Jack turned around and watched the last few words come from the chapped lips of an old woman who had just entered the room. She looked so much older than Nanna Tess, if that were at all possible. Two tiny black pearl eyes set deep into dark sockets caught the dim candlelight and glowed eerily. Jack could not help but stare into them distracted for a moment from the line of warts that grew on the left side of her crooked nose. There was something about her gaze that he felt compelled to look into them. He tried to look away but he could not even though they scared him.

"Thank you..." Jack managed to say, quite lost for words but struggling to be polite. He did not know this old woman and for that matter neither did Martha.

She held out a hand and Jack studied it, noticing immediately, the skinny bones beneath the pale translucent skin, and the blood running through the tortuous blue veins that travelled all the way down to her thick crumbling yellowed nails. He knew he was still staring at her hand for a very long time and began to notice the uncomfortable pause. He had no choice but to shake the hand offered to him. Jack's heart began to beat faster and a cold sweat broke out across his brow. He took her hand. What struck him the most was her touch. Jack had held Nanna Tess' hand when he'd found her and he knew it hadn't been like this. This woman's touch couldn't have been any colder if she herself were dead and risen from the grave.

"Oh, where are my manners dear boy?" she asked half cackling half coughing to herself. She didn't even bother to put a hand over her mouth either and Jack gagged from the foul smell of her breath; a mix of rotten onions and stagnant water, it could strip the varnish off a ship's deck he thought. The last time he'd smelled something as vile was when he stood face to face with the Shimnavore in Annalong Wood.

He shivered at the thought.

"I am a very old and a very dear friend of your late Nanna Tess. We used to play together as children back in the poor house..." She gasped at what she'd said and decided now was a good time to cover her mouth. "I'm ever so sorry. I meant orphanage... Tess and I used to play together as children back at the orphanage." Her ploy to cover up her mistake seemed obvious to Jack. What was she playing at?

Next she extended her hand to Martha.

Jack glanced over to his mother but she looked just as bewildered. All either of them knew of Nanna Tess' past was what she'd told them and it certainly didn't involve being an orphan. Tess had often spoken of parents and happy times. Was it all a lie and if so why had she hidden the truth from them?

Martha reached out and shook the old woman's hand. Jack's eyes widened as he noticed his mother flinch just as he had done. He wondered if his mother had noticed how cold the old woman's skin was just like he had but it seemed more than that. A deep worry-line stretched across Martha's forehead and Jack sensed that his mother was somehow in pain. He could also tell that she was trying desperately to hide that pain from him.

"I'm afraid Tess never spoke of you Mrs...Mrs..." Martha paused for a moment, trying not to make it too obvious that she was fishing for a name.

"Misssss! It is Missssss..." she hissed. "Misssss Doolen." She withdrew her hand with lightning speed. "I'm surprised Tess never spoke of me. She promised she would leave me a gift when she died and you say she never mentioned this?"

Something didn't ring true. Jack knew a lie when he heard one and this woman was lying through her black teeth, all three of them. But why would an old woman do such a thing?

"If you don't mind me asking, what was the gift?" asked Martha.

"Oh, just a silly trinket, almost too small to even mention." Miss Doolen waved her horrid hand dismissively. "More sentimental value than anything you understand."

"Can you describe it? Maybe I'd have a better idea," asked Martha.

"It was a flower-shaped locket. The top of it was like a small spiky ball. It was unusual because it had two chains instead of one. Tess never took it off her and she knew I admired it so and that was when she promised me that it would be mine if she died before I did."

Jack noticed the old woman shift uncomfortably as she spoke. She looked down at him and tried to smile but it held the same warmth as her hand and a chill ran down his back. He instinctively reached up and clasped his mother's hand squeezing it for all he was worth.

"I'm afraid I really don't know what you're talking about," Martha said, hiding the pain of her son crushing her hand. "But I assure you if I come across anything like that I will let you know. Do you live close by?"

A wrinkled eyelid eclipsed the tiny dark eyeball as the old lady attempted a wink and she flicked an oversized wart at the tip of her nose with a bony finger. "I'm never too far away Martha…never too far."

When she finished speaking, she turned on her heels and made a hasty retreat. Hasty- the old hag moved like a five-year old being chased in a school playground.

Jack thought she looked like she'd just lost an important battle, one that they, the Turner's, had won.

Chapter 2

Who's that at this hour?

Soon after the old hag Doolen left the cottage, the rest of the mourners followed. Martha had insisted that only she and Jack were to stay with Tess on her last night. There were tuts and shakes of heads from the older women and even a word or two was spoken about evil spirits from those feeling aggrieved at being asked to go.   By midnight, the cottage was in silence.

Jack stood at the hearth heating a tin pot of tea to bring in to his mother. On occasions such as this, even he was allowed to have a cup. Nanna Tess had kept a tea caddy on the shelf above her chair and no one, not even Jack's Da, dared touch it. Now that Tess had passed, Jack knew she wouldn't mind, if anything she'd encourage it.

"Ma, who was that woman?" shouted Jack, a tremor in his voice from just thinking of her.

"I don't know Jack but I know one thing for sure, she scared the wits out of me," Martha replied, her voice low enough to be respectful to Tess but loud enough for her son to hear.

Jack knew exactly what she'd meant. He had just returned from the most amazing adventure of his life and had experienced things that most people would never experience even if they lived a hundred lifetimes. He had feared for his life and been scared beyond belief but this time was very different, this time it happened in his realm, the Outer Realm and in his own home no less, where bad magic didn't exist.

Or did it?

Jack brought a wooden tray, holding the best china cup, in to his mother and he gave it to her then he sat on a small wicker chair in the corner and began to sip his. The taste of the tea instantly flooded his mind with wonderful memories of Nanna Tess, rare times when Tess would open the tea caddy. It was usually a special birthday, maybe an anniversary, Christmas, or that one time when his brother Edmund...

A furious pounding at the front door suddenly disturbed the absolute silence in the wake house. The sound startled Jack and he yelped and let his cup fly.

It smashed against the wall. Jack watched the tea stream down onto the floor. He blushed with embarrassment at the high pitched sound he had just made and from the sight of the now broken cup.

"Who on earth could that be at this hour?" shouted Martha. "Don't they have any respect for a wake house?"

Goosebumps erupted all over Jack's arms but he didn't want to look any more frightened than he already was to his mother. He stood up and puffed out his chest trying to show that he now was the man of the house. He so wanted his mother to be proud of him and let her know that he could protect her. He had raised an army of evil creatures, marched underground through miles of tunnel, and defeated a Shimnavore; surely, he could do something as simple as answer his own front door.

The incessant hammering became even more urgent.

"I'll go," Jack said. "It's so dark out; whoever it is probably hasn't seen the wreath on the door."

Jack left Tess' room, went quickly across to the hearth in the living room, and lifted the poker. He didn't know what he was supposed to do with it but somehow it made him feel a little safer.

From the mighty bangs coming from the door Jack knew that whoever was on the other side was kicking and punching it for all they were worth.

"Who's there?" shouted Jack.

The knocking stopped but no reply came.

"Whoever it is, don't you know this is a wake house. Now have some respect and leave," said Jack. He'd lowered and deepened his voice trying to make him sound older. No sooner had he finished speaking when the knocking started again only this time much stronger and with even more anger. Jack watched helplessly as the latch on the door bent under the force. It didn't look like it would hold much longer. He glanced down to the poker in his shaking hand. It didn't seem like a weapon that would be of any use once the thing on the other side of the door broke in. His eyes darted into every darkened corner of the room hoping beyond hope that there might be see something bigger than the poker, but there wasn't. The longer the pounding went on the more Jack let his imagination get the better of him. He had visions of Shimnavore and creatures conjured up from his worst nightmare trying to gain entry to his home. He quickly convinced himself that it was impossible but an irrational mind is difficult to calm.

Whatever it was outside, both he and his mother were at its mercy.

"Open this door right now Jack Turner or so help me I'll kick it in."

Jack's heart skipped a beat. He recognised the voice. It was old man Russell, the Fishmonger, the man who had bought the fish from his father for as long as he could remember. But what on earth was he doing out at such an hour? Jack hurried to the door and lifted the latch. It burst open with such force Jack was thrown against the wall, winding him. He sank to his knees, fighting to catch the stolen breath from his lungs, and watched in disbelief as six strong fishermen strode into the cottage. They were drenched and dripped salt water all over the floor but Jack had no time to complain for what they were holding on their shoulders caused him to yell out.

"Ma, come quick."

Jack grabbed his knees tightly to his chest, still holding the poker and stared in disbelief as a lifeless body, arms limp and outstretched, was set down on the kitchen table.

It was his father.

Chapter 3

Dead or alive

Jack had wished for his father's return, but not like this. This was something from a nightmare, something far beyond his control.

Martha came out of Tess' room, and stood in disbelief at the sight unfolding in front of her eyes. When the reality of what was happening hit her she ran to her husband and clasped his icy cold hand.

"He's been gone for days now," she wailed, rocking back and forth. She began to sob uncontrollably. "He's dead. I know he is."

"Calm yourself Martha." Old man Russell grabbed her shoulders and spoke directly into her face. "Matthew is not dead but he is very close. He's just been found on the rocks of Haulbowline lighthouse, miles from where we found his boat. How he managed to get there is a mystery to us all but a welcome one. The cold has got to him and he's just about clinging on to life."

Martha released herself from Russell's hold, pressed her face close to Matthew's, and pleaded for him to hang on. She looked back to her son and stretched out her hand. Jack willed his legs to move but they wouldn't budge. An invisible force had pinned him to the wall and he knew that force all too well. It was fear itself. He fought hard to get up. He remembered the night in Annalong Wood as the fearsome Shimnavore came tearing towards him, the sight of his own blood as he stared at the gaping wound next to his heart. All these were real. They happened in the Inner Realm but somehow this was different, this was in his realm: a realm where magic did not exist. Then the sight of two tiny black pearl eyes flashed into his mind and Mrs Doolen's face stared right at him. Why should he think of her at such a time? And why did he think she had something to do with what was going on right now?

Magic indeed.

Jack took a deep breath and struggled to his feet. He reached out his hand and stumbled towards the dinner table grabbing the trouser leg of his father as he was about to fall.

"Will he live Ma?" he asked, not wanting an honest answer.

"We'd best get him out of these wet things and into his bed." Martha replied. "I know where Tess' balm is to rub into his chest to help his breathing."

Jack had never been more proud of his mother. She had set aside her emotions and taken control of the situation. He knew she was a strong woman and even worked in the Old Mill when she was younger but he had never seen her act like that before. The men surrounded Matthew and lifted him into his room and Martha followed closely behind. They laid him on his bed, left the room and the last one closed the door.

Old man Russell sat down next to Jack who was staring into the fire embers just as Nanna Tess had done many a night. Jack could feel his fingers open as Mr Russell prised the poker from his tight grip.

"It'll be alright son, you mark my words. Good things happen to good people and your father is one of the best."

Jack felt a warmth flow through him, it was an enormous swell of pride hearing someone speak so highly of his father, but it still didn't quell his worst fear.

As Jack tried to make sense of what was happening a roar came from inside his parent's room. He sprang to his feet, ignoring the pain in his back from hitting the wall, and dashed into the room. His father was sitting bolt upright in his bed, arms outstretched, eyes bulging in his head. Then his mouth opened and the words came pouring out. It was as though he were not speaking them with his mouth or lips but that they were flowing up from deep within him.

"EREAF MAY OULAS."

The voice did not sound like his father's but who else's could it have been? By now all the fishermen were gathered round the bedroom door peering in. They stared in disbelief when they saw Matthew sitting upright. Not one of them could believe that a man on the brink of death could have this much fight left in him but the words he uttered, although they were completely incomprehensible, left every man who heard him speak with a sudden inexplicable chill. It was like an army had just marched over all their graves.

The words Matthew spoke were incomprehensible, of course they were, that is unless you were a certain boy who'd been given a certain potion to drink by a certain Clurichaun. Matthew's words had not fallen on deaf ears. Could he have known that Jack would have understood them? Did he even understand Jack was in the same room?

Jack had understood the words his father had spoken all right, for every hair on his body stood up when he heard them. But now he found it hard to think straight. What could he do? Who could he turn to? He could confide in no one for they would think him mad and this helplessness scared him to his very core.

Chapter 4

Alone

By two o'clock in the morning the men left Jack's cottage and the house was once again left in peace. Jack could see that his mother was torn in her duty' to sit with Nanna Tess on her last night on the earth, before she would be beneath it and staying with her husband to nurse him in whatever way she could.

"I am going to sit with Nanna Tess Ma alright. Da needs you more," explained Jack. He could see the sense of relief on her face and he hid the sense of dread from his. It would give him time to think, time to make a plan. But he had no idea what he would or even could do. His father lay at death's door and his Nanna Tess had just passed through it but not in the traditional sense. There was no one he could talk to, no one to confide in. The best friend he had ever made was a world and a year away. It would be too long to wait until his next birthday but he had little choice.

But Jack was the last of the Elderfolk; he knew he had to come up with something.

Jack gave a last glance over his shoulder at his mother lying next to his father, stroking his hair and whispering to him. He could guess what she was saying to him for if he were there he would be telling him to fight for just long enough until he could rescue him and rescue him he would. It was a promise he had made. It would never be broken.

Nanna Tess's room had a soft honeyed glow when he entered and it should have put him at ease but it didn't. The troubles in the other room seemed to grow in his head and it began to throb. The faint air of honeysuckle no longer lingered, replaced by a very bad smell. It came from the direction of the window as if carried in on the night air. Jack noticed the curtain lifting in the breeze. Someone had opened the window. But that was not possible. Jack thought hard. Had one of the fishermen entered the room? There was that much commotion earlier maybe one of them did. Jack closed the window but when he turned back into the room, he could see Tess' hands were open and her red rose was lying crushed on the floor.

Jack's eyes widened at the sight. An anger began to well up inside him. Someone had the gall to enter his Nanna's resting place.

He sat on the edge of her bed staring at the window. His mind ached with the thoughts and emotions bursting to get out. Finally, he turned to Tess and began to speak.

"I don't know if you can hear me Nanna, but if even a wee bit can I just want you to know that you are one of my greatest heroes. You prepared me for the greatest journey of my life but now I need you more than ever. Help me Nanna."

Jack looked up at the bare wall knowing his parents lay beyond it. He could envisage his father's chest rising and falling with such effort.

The words he had spoken swirled around in his head.

'Ereaf May Oulas.'

He understood them the instant they were uttered but what they meant scared him. 'Free my soul,' his father had implored. Wherever his father was he was not in the house, part of him lay elsewhere, a place Jack couldn't begin to imagine. The only place Jack had ever felt safe was at home by his father's side or in his own special hiding place in the Old Mill.

But what could he do to help his father now? Someone had the answer and at least he knew where to start for the smell of her foul breath lingered around him. He would find the answer tomorrow at Tess' funeral. There was one person who knew more than she was letting on.

A fine drizzle descended from dark skies the morning of the funeral and all gathered bowed their heads as Tess was lowered into the ground. Jack stood alone, his mother had to stay with his father, this he understood but their absence filled him with emptiness.

Then he spied her from the corner of his eye, the old hag Doolen. The more he looked at her the more he knew she was up to no good. He was convinced she'd been in his Nanna's room the night before and dared to touch her body.

After the funeral, as everyone turned to leave, Jack approached the old woman.

"I know where you were last night," said Jack.

Old Miss Doolen stared right through Jack as if he wasn't there.

"Be very careful how you talk to me dear one." She wagged a gnarled finger into his face. "A stone can only work so many times on a boy."

The words shook Jack. How could she have known about the Obsidian black Stone let alone what magic it had held for both him and his Nanna Tess? He gulped before he spoke again.

"I still know where you were last night. You were obviously searching for something but I know you didn't find it or you wouldn't be here today. Whatever it is I will make sure you never get your bony claws on it."

Jack turned on his heels to leave but he couldn't for standing right in front of him, blocking him, was the old hag. It wasn't possible. She was just behind him. There was no way she could... He turned again and there she stood. He turned repeatedly but each time she was blocking his escape. His heart pounded in his chest and beads of cold sweat ran down his brow. Who was this creature? She certainly couldn't be human. Was she something disguised as an old woman? thought Jack.

"You listen to me you young imp, I will get what I am seeking, I've raised a storm trying to get what I want and you or no power on this earth will stop me. Not even Blianta could stop me."

Jack had no idea who or what Blianta was but couldn't take it any longer; he couldn't listen to another word coming from her foul mouth. He needed to get far away from the hag. The courage he had built up to confront her had almost left him but hearing her mention the storm gave him a renewed vigour. He closed his eyes and he kicked hard hoping his boot would connect with her bony shin. It didn't hit anything. He opened his eyes and looked over his shoulder as he dashed away but to his astonishment there was no one there. The heath was empty except for a tilted tombstone in the distance and a strange swirling black cloud.

Once Jack thought he was a far enough away from the graveyard he stopped running. There was no way she could catch him now he convinced himself and he began to traipse the rest of the way back home with a heart that weighed heavy in his chest. He began to think of Nanna Tess, she had been a constant in his life, someone who had always been there, someone he could talk to when he couldn't share something with his mother or father. He entered the cottage quietly and made straight for his parent's room but the scene remained unchanged. His mother lay on the bed next to his Da stroking his hair and whispering into his ear.

Jack closed the bedroom door, went to his own room and lay on his bed. He stared up at the rafters and in his mind's eye, he could make out shapes in the thatch that soon melted together to become faces, like lying on a hillside and looking up at moving clouds. The face that appeared the most was Nanna Tess', but she was gone now and he had to figure out a way to help his Da all by himself.

Thinking of his Da made him remember what the Hag had said. She had told Jack she had even raised a storm trying to get what she wanted. Had she created the storm that nearly took his Da's life? Was she trying to get to his Nanna Tess through his father? But Tess was dead now and Jack knew from the state his father was in that wouldn't be long before he would be returning to the graveyard for another funeral...And the very thought of it pained him. He closed his eyes and it wasn't long before they began to flicker under his eyelids as he fell into a deep sleep.

Chapter 5

Freedom

A rush of air and an explosion of light filled Jack with an exhilaration that reached deep into his heart. He could not explain the sudden weightlessness, the sudden power at his disposal but it was the greatest thrill of his short life. The sky was azure blue and cloudless with a golden flaming sun but Jack cast no shadow for he was not on the ground. He was soaring high above the Mountains of Mourne, swooping headlong and hitting warm currents of air that lifted him even higher. He screamed out in joy but nothing came from his throat except a shrill caw.

That's when he spied it, a field mouse, clinging onto a reed by the side of a lake far below. The hunger inside overwhelmed Jack and he plunged down at tremendous speed, diving towards his prey like a thunderbolt. The ground rushed up to meet him and Jack could see two strong talons beneath him outstretched ready to grab the mouse. Jack caught his reflection on the lake and suddenly realised he was in a dream. His blue grey wings were outstretched and he could make out a pale neck and throat. The white underbelly gave it away. Jack was a peregrine falcon about to catch his mouse. But this mouse didn't want to be caught today and he bolted into a nearby hole. Just as he was about to crash into the embankment the wings subtly moved and instantly he soared back into the sky.

Dreams had never been this real before. Jack could taste blood in his mouth from a previous kill and for some strange reason it was good. He had a heightened sense of awareness. A sense that he was connected to everything going on around him unlike anything he had ever experienced before.

The dream lasted for hours and Jack covered the length and breadth of the mountain range; from the slopes of Pollaphuca to the mighty heights of Slieve Donard and from the crystal waters of Fofanny Dam to the breath taking scenes of Carlingford Lough, always searching, always hungry. But finally the bird rested in a nook high up in a rocky cliff on the side of Slieve Martin. As the bird began to fall asleep Jack opened his eyes. He was awake.

Instead of the sunlight steaming in through the curtains there was darkness. No wait…a moving shadow… two black pearls of eerie light were looking through the window. A sudden chill ran through Jack's body and instinctively he pulled the patchwork quilt up over his head. Something or someone was watching him sleep. Although a fear gripped his heart Jack managed to pluck up the courage to confront whoever or whatever it was looking in at him. But the second he threw off the quilt the eyes at the window vanished.

Jack ran to the window and looked out but apart from the sheets, hanging on the line there was no one to be seen. He climbed back into bed and lay there trying to make sense of it all. He had fallen asleep at noon and had the most amazing dream of his life. In his dream, he had spent the day as a bird flying over the mountains. The very memory made his heart speed up. It had been so real. He hadn't been in control; at best, it could be described as being a passenger in another creature's body. But the length of time was weirdest of all. In a normal nap you don't wake up and the day is gone. There was something much more to this but Jack couldn't work out what. The strangest thing too was that he was exhausted. He had slept the whole day but now he was awake he felt more tired than he had when he nodded off in the first place.

There was only one thing left to do and that was to go back to sleep. The image at the window stared back at him as soon as his eyelids closed and he quickly opened them again. Jack convinced himself they had been a figment of his imagination, what with everything that had gone on the past few days he allowed himself to be a bit out of sorts. He stared up into the darkness and soon his eyelids began to weigh heavy until he could keep them open no longer.

The sweet smell of damp earth filled his nostrils and his nose twitched incessantly as his fine long hairs touched the rough walls. Even in the pitch black Jack could make out the grimy walls of a burrow. Wherever his dream had taken him this time he knew he was deep underground.

Wait…

What was that up ahead? A small glimmer of light. The tiny paws beneath him scurried toward it and within moments, he was in an underground burrow but his was no ordinary burrow; this was lavishly furnished with tables and chairs and bookshelves from floor to ceiling. It had windows but they were quite literally placed on the mud walls with a painting of Slieve Donard behind the panes of glass. Heavy green velvet curtains framed them. Under his bare feet were rugs of beautifully patterned scenes of the Mourne Mountains. Jack recognised the peaks of Commedagh and Bearnagh, embroidered in such detail, the green hues of the fields and ruddy browns of the hills. Whoever created these had great patience and skill.

The table, covered with a fine linen tablecloth was set for breakfast and a small silver candelabra with long bright red candles illuminated the china cups and plates. They too depicted the rivers and valleys of the Mourne Mountains. Silk napkins inside silver rings gleamed in the half-light and a ruby red bowl filled with fruit sat in pride of place in the centre.

Jack could feel the nose of the creature twitch as the smell cooking wafted in from another room. He heard a clanking of pots and pans.

"Sorrell Speedwell I hope your paws are clean, your breakfast is almost ready," a friendly female voice shouted from what Jack presumed to be the kitchen.

As his head moved downward Jack could make out two grimy paws with filthy claws, short and sharp looking back up at him. He went over to a basin of water and washed the dirt away and started to dry his paws.

"If you're drying your hands on your shirt again so help me I'll…" the voice called again only this time not so friendly.

Jack could sense a flush of guilt as it flowed through the body he was inside as two, now clean; paws stuffed his shirttails into his britches. A voice interrupted, soft with just a hint of gravel.

"Sorry mama." Sorrell Speedwell knew better than to lie to his mother and Jack could sense this. He could feel

Sorrell's heart skip. He was a passenger in another body again and although it wasn't as exciting as being a peregrine falcon it certainly was more entertaining.

Hold on a moment, Sorrell was moving over to a full-length mirror to check to see if his mother would approve of his appearance for breakfast.

Standing there was a small immaculately dressed white mole, but not a mole. Jack had never seen anything like this creature before. He was a rotund ball of fur and wore a tweed three-piece suit as if he were ready to go somewhere terribly important. A reddish pink handkerchief poked out of his top pocket and it matched the colour of his dickey bow. The edges of his collar and cuffs were feathery and frayed.

Sorrell Speedwell was from a long and proud race of thieving Bogbeans, a curious race of underground pick pocketing dwellers who were sticklers for ceremony, only Sorrell didn't seem to share in their sense of occasion. He liked nothing better than being armpit deep in a mud bank searching for grubs. He sat at the table and waited for his breakfast to arrive.

Sorrell's mother entered the room holding a large silver tray but when she saw her son, she screamed out, "Sorrell, what's happened to your eyes?" She let go of the tray and it went crashing onto the table sending the scalding herbal tea all over Sorrell's arm. Sorrell had such a fright he jumped up with the agonising pain searing through his arm and at that precise moment, Jack awoke with a start.

Outside Jack's window, two black pearl eyes glowed eerily in the early morning twilight.

Chapter 6

Tomb

In a dark corner of Annalong graveyard where daylight never seemed to reach there lay a tomb carved with great detail and it depicted a ship of stone flying in the clouds over a stormy sea. But not all was as it seemed for if you looked carefully you could see the earth surrounding the tomb had been moved. It was as if the tomb's lid had slid sideways to let something enter or even worse, let something leave and that something was approaching, floating off the ground, travelling at lightning speed. Like a cloud of darkness, it swept over the gravestones until it came to stop at the tomb. The name carved on the headstone read Doolen.

The cloud of darkness was actually a huge swarm of tiny black winged insects and they began to swirl round like a small hurricane and as it spun, it began to take solid form. With a sweep of a withered pale hand the tombstone began to move all by itself and slowly a set of stone steps revealed themselves leading down into the earth. The darkness had transformed into the old hag Doolen and she descended into the depths of the tomb cursing to herself. She had not found what she needed and now the sun was rising she had no option but to hide. She could only stay in the light for very short periods of time as it drained her energy.

Her thoughts were dark, they dwelled on one person, and that was Jack Tuner. He had the answer, she knew it, but how could she prise it from him? She was weaker than she had ever been. It took a lot of power to muster up a spell strong enough to command the elements and create the biggest storm Ireland had ever seen. From deep within her tomb that night, she could see the image of the small boat in her huge cauldron with Matthew at the helm tossed around like a child's toy on the rough seas. She witnessed the capsizing of the boat and held her breath as it dashed against the rocks. She watched with a wide grin on her crooked mouth as the ghostly-white mist lifted from Matthew's body. But something was not right, his image disappeared from the cauldron as if a power stronger than hers was blocking him from her sight and she knew only one person had that power but now she was dead, buried that very morning. There was nothing stopping her now. The spell over the cottage would wear off now that Tess had died and soon Doolen could enter and leave as she pleased.

She knew Matthew's soul was somewhere in the other realm but the shock of seeing his body being lifted into the cottage at Tess's wake only made her more enraged. Something had caused him to be hidden from her sight the night of the storm and he hadn't fallen into the depths of the sea. But what power could protect him like this? No wonder her plan had been foiled. No mortal man could live without his life force but this was no ordinary man. It would only be a matter of time before the body of this Elderfolk perished, and then his soul would be truly free from its shackles.

Her plan had taken many lifetimes to achieve since cast into the Outer Realm. It had taken two thousand years trying to find the descendants of the Elderfolk. They were integral to her plan for draining their life force; the soul of an Elderfolk was the only way the very fabric between worlds could be torn.

But now she questioned the need for Matthew's soul for she had sensed something cataclysmic had happened in the InBetween and the Inner Realm. Not since the Holocene had she experienced such a feeling. She knew the Orb was shattered and the walls had fallen for she could hear her master in her thoughts for the first time in two millennia. But the breaking of the Orb to the Inner Realm had nothing to do with Matthew. In the very moment the Orb shattered she had a vision. In her vision she saw that a boy called Jack Turner had found the secret of the Silver Orb. He held a power so mighty he could bring down the walls between the InBetween and the Outer Realm.

Was it possible she had chosen the wrong person to raise the storm against? If Matthew was not the chosen one there was only one person left. She hadn't considered such a puny weakling. How could the soul of a boy hold more power than his father? Matthew was as strong a man as she ever had seen but now she knew it didn't mean that the life force that flowed inside him equalled the actual size of his body.

The more the old hag thought about the InBetween the more she longed to be back with her kind again and take her rightful place as queen.

She would bide her time, for time was on her side; over two thousand years had seemed like an eternity in the Outer Realm. The very thought of her exile filled her with bitterness. Her kind had been driven mad on their long journey to Ireland's shores across the vast treacherous oceans of time but her madness was now only equalled by her wickedness.

She could smell success was near. At worst, all she needed was to get her hands on the necklace, the Talisman, and at best, Jack Turner's death.

Chapter 7

The Eyes

Jack could not stop the screams of Sorrell's mother echoing in his mind. What scared her so when she had looked at her son? Jack knew it was just a dream but the sensations he felt, the smells, sounds and the terrible pain from the scalding hot tea. He looked at his left arm and his eyes widened when he saw a huge red blister. He touched it and flinched with the pain. It was not possible. A dream couldn't hurt you. Could it? Something must have happened. Jack glanced over to his bedside locker and he felt a sense of relief when he saw an overturned candle. He convinced himself he must have knocked it over whilst he slept. He put such thoughts from his mind, thoughts like not remembering lighting a candle in the first place or the fact that there wasn't any candle wax on his arm.

The overwhelming tiredness remained and Jack thought he must have been coming down with something, a summer cold perhaps. His Nanna would have had answers for him and he knew it was no good asking his mother for she had worries of her own.

Jack dragged himself from his bed and went to check on his parents. Sure enough, Martha was beside Matthew staring at him and Jack could see the look of despair on her face.

"Ma, he will get better, ya know," lied Jack. He couldn't think of anything else to say except, "you must be famished, let me fix you something to eat."

"It's all right son, sure I'm not that hungry anyway."

"But you haven't eaten and you need all your strength. That's what you're always telling me."

"All right son maybe a bit of soda farl and a wee cup a' tea."

"I'll get it right away." Jack turned to leave and as he did so he could hear his mother whisper to his Da, "you raised a good one there Matthew. I couldn't be more proud of the boy."

Jack could not take the smile off his face as he made breakfast. To hear his mother speak like that filled him with such a sense of pride. He would do everything he could to help his father. All he needed was a plan. Oh, and a good days sleep.

Jack took the breakfast tray into his mother and sat it on the side of the bed. She instantly noticed the burn on his arm.

"What on earth happened to you?"

"Nothing, I just spilled some candle wax on it."

"Well make sure you put some of Nanna Tess' salve on it. It'll cure it in no time. Oh and I'm so sorry Jack, my mind has been so far away. How was the funeral?"

"More than half the village was there Ma. There were some very nice things said about her. There wasn't a single person she hadn't helped out in one way or another. If Old Doc Chambers couldn't fix them then they knew Tess would have the answer. And that came from Doc Chambers' own mouth. He said he'd love to have been privy to her recipes. He called her an old witch and everyone laughed."

Jack could not help but notice his mother's face flush.

"He meant it as a joke Ma."

Martha sat up on the bed and tried to compose herself. "Of course he did Jack, of course he did. By the way... you have large dark rings under your eyes. Are you sleeping alright?" she said partly out of concern but more to change the subject.

"Yeah, loads in fact. But here's the weird thing, the more I sleep the more tired I feel. If ya really want to know...I'm   exhausted."

"Oh I hate when that happens. You should go out for a walk and clear your head. It always works for me and when you're out perhaps you'll bring some flowers to your Nanna's grave. What with everything that happened I didn't get the chance. Pick some flowers from the garden. I know she'd like that."

Jack sat in the garden and looked at all the flowers in bloom. Nanna Tess had planted every one of them. Wild roses, forget-me-nots, sweet pea were all her favourites so Jack put together a small posy. Why he hadn't done it the day before he didn't know. Too many things were going on in his mind, a dead great grandmother who he admired so dearly, and a father who was clinging on to life. He knew he had the answer somewhere deep inside him but he did not know how to find it.

The walk to the graveyard was pleasant. The smell of the wild roses always reminded him of being a very young child playing in the garden under the watchful eye of his Nanna. His mother was always working, scrubbing clothes, preparing dinner, mending nets. He especially loved the way his mother never grumbled. He knew she had a hard life, what with the death of his brother Edmund and all. But if ever there was a true hero it was her. She took on every task with a willingness that deeply impressed him. If only he grew up with a fraction of her 'get up and go' then he knew he'd turn out all right.

The earth was fresh at his Nanna's plot and the headstone had been removed. It was off getting Nanna's name carved onto it beneath that of her husband's. Jack laid the posy of flowers onto the ground next to the others and then lay down on the warm grass and looked up at the sun.

"Nanna Tess, if ever I needed your help now is the time."

Jack closed his eyes for a moment, the tiredness he'd fought so hard all morning was beginning to take its toll but he couldn't drift off to sleep. He put his hand out and lifted some of the fresh earth from Tess' grave. The warm dry soil fell between his fingers and Jack thought of the sands of time his father had often mentioned. 'Never regret the mistakes you make,' he would say, 'you only learn from them.' Jack still didn't know what it meant but somehow it made him feel better. Still he couldn't nod off. It was almost as if the only place he could sleep was in his own bed. Reluctantly he got up and with great effort; he made his way home and fell onto his bed. Within seconds of his head hitting the pillow he was fast asleep.

Chapter 8

I know it's you

Tumbling...spinning... churning...

Jack fell deeper and deeper into the murky depths. The walls of an embankment flitted by in a haze of muddy brown. Water flooded into his lungs but to his utter surprise he wasn't drowning. Instead he was taking in huge mouthfuls of the stuff... breathing in the liquid... breathing underwater just like a fish. Silver scales danced all around him, flitting one way, darting another. This time he was inside the body of a fish. Jack belonged to a huge school of fish; Scaden to be more precise.

Another amazing dream he thought.

He had soared and conquered the skies of the Mournes, dug deep and burrowed beneath them but by far the strangest sensation was to swim in her rivers. If only he knew whether he was in a river, a lake, or a stream. It was all so new. The body he inhabited was so nimble, a flick of a fin, a swish of a tail and he careered to the left or right. The fish Jack inhabited was young; he could sense that, just learning to keep up with all those surrounding him. But what was that up ahead, behind the reeds, green and gold shimmering in the light? The young fish knew instinctively it had to escape for bearing down on him with an evil grin full of fangs... oh no... a giant pike. Huge malicious eyes stared right at him, unfaltering. He had been singled out and it was only a matter of time before he would meet his untimely end. Even at such a young age, this small creature knew it was not destined to be long on the earth. The pike's mouth opened wide... wide enough for Jack to realise where he was going to end up.   The pike's sharp teeth snapped shut...

"Ahhhh."

Jack awoke with a sharp pain in his head. He threw his hands up and felt along his hairline. There were indentations in his skin. He got up, rushed to the small mirror on his locker, and lifted back his hair. Tooth marks, on the sides of his temples were reflected back at him. They weren't there before he went to bed. Somehow, the thought of the candle wax burning his arm didn't seem so convincing now. No... his mind was playing tricks on him. They couldn't be tooth marks. That was just stupid. He'd fallen asleep on the pillow and somehow the folds of cloth had pressed against him making the indentations like teeth. Jack had been in such a deep sleep he hadn't roused until the dream became so nightmarish he could stand it no longer. But he couldn't be afraid of a nightmare especially when the sun beat, so invitingly, in through the window. One more sleep wouldn't hurt.

"Wheeeeeeeeeeeeeeeeeeeeeeeeeeeeee."

A joyous voice cried out and the heart of whomever Jack inhabited this time was beating faster than a drum roll. He could see a pair of shiny boots sticking straight up into the air with red and green stripy socks poking out of them. His head grew dizzy as he fell, spinning round and round, getting faster and faster with every turn until he crashed into a huge pillow. It burst on impact, a flurry of white feathers exploded all around him, and the sounds of laughter filled the air. Jack had just come down a huge helter skelter attached to a spiral staircase. This wasn't his first experience of the staircase and the familiarity immediately drove away the thoughts of his previous fishy nightmare. Jack knew where he was.

Once the room finally decided to stop moving, the body Jack was now inside stood up and crossed to a doorway. He looked out and through his eyes Jack could see a whole family of people gathered around a large oak table. There were ten in all and every one of them wore a distinctive waistcoat. They looked as though they were getting ready for a great banquet. Bunting hung from the branches of every tree and in the open paddock four white tents, as big as Jack's cottage, held even more tables. From the scene in front of him it was obvious to Jack that more guests were expected.

Just as Jack was about to step outside a hand grabbed him by his belt and dragged him back inside.

"It's you Jack Turner. I just know it is."

"What are you talking about? Now just let me go. I know it's been a while and being alone in this big old house has played tricks with your mind but my name is Fearnog remember?"

"Just shut up for a minute Fearnog, I'm not talking to you. I'm talking to who is inside of you," said Cobs.

Fearnog looked puzzled. His brother had obviously lost his mind. Cobs continued to talk.

"Just as you stepped off the helter skelter I caught a glimpse of your eyes. Fearnog's eyes are sky blue and his pupils are long. Your eyes Jack, well they're dark brown, as dark as coal and as brown as mahogany. I'd know them in a heartbeat."

Jack could sense Fearnog's frustration but it wasn't half as bad as his own. Standing in front of him in resplendent new clothes of the finest quality was the best friend he had ever known. His waistcoat was no longer dull, instead it was so colourful with its golds and greens and a shirt so dazzlingly white Jack nearly blinked. The trousers he wore were blood red with not a patch in sight. But one thing remained untouched, the huge hat with the green bandana still adorned his head.

Cobs was the most welcome sight in all the world.

He stood talking to him and all he could do was…. well… nothing. Jack remained helpless, caught, trapped inside a body he had no control over.

"Jack. I know you can hear me," said Cobs, holding Fearnog's shoulders.

Fearnog pulled away but Cobs grabbed him tightly and smacked him hard across the face.

"Oi what'd ya do that for?" said Fearnog rubbing his cheek.

"I'm sorry Fearnog but you have to trust me. You have to believe me. Just do me this one small favour. Sit down and stay still."

After all Cobs had done for him and the whole Hawksbeard clan Fearnog couldn't refuse his brother. He would indulge Cobs just this once. Cobs leaned in close and whispered into his brother's pointed ear.

"I know it's you Jack. As soon as I saw those eyes, I knew it couldn't be anyone else."

Jack could not believe it. Cobs was sitting right in front of him and he knew he was Jack Turner but in Fearnog's body.

"I didn't think this would happen so soon Jack but there you go. Jack, there can only be one explanation for all this. You must be sleeping on the Talisman or at least half of it anyway."

Cobs could see desperation in Jack's eyes. He knew something terrible must have happened and he would do everything in his power to help his friend. He continued to speak.

"The Talisman holds great power. It once belonged to someone known only as Salix. No one knows what Salix originally looked like or where he came from but it was said that he could move like a mist, travel great distances then once he found a host he could take over their body, and control them from the inside like a puppeteer controlling a puppet. They call it Dream Walking. It is where your mind leaves your body and can go into someone else's. You can see through their eyes and feel everything they feel. But your own body lies dormant so it cannot be left forever or it will die and your spirit will be trapped in whoever you have taken over. But legend also has it that Salix came upon a race of Bogbeans and he liked the way they lived so much, their pomp and ceremony, their thieving mischief that he decided to stay in the body of someone known as Teirnan Speedwell."

Jack's eyes grew larger when he heard the name Speedwell. That was the name called out from the kitchen in the underground burrow. It couldn't be just a coincidence, could it?

Cobs continued. "Somehow Salix lost the Talisman. I personally think he didn't return to his own body and he died. The Talisman was found but many battles were fought over it until finally it found its way into the hands of the Sisters of the Heather and they, realising its true and dangerous nature, swore to protect it. They promised it would never be used again."

Cobs breathed in deeply and then sighed. He blew a steady stream of air from his lips then he began his confession. "What I am about to tell you is very hard but please understand I did it for my family. I happened upon the Talisman Jack, I'll not say how for it is not something I am terribly proud of. Let's just say it was a good enough reason for Erica Tetralix never to talk to me again. Once I had the Talisman I couldn't wait to wear it. I wanted to see through the eyes of all the creatures in the Mournes to find my family. I knew someone must have known where they went that day. The darkest day of my life, the day they never came home but alas, it was not to be. I had a few near scrapes with death myself while I wore the Talisman I can tell ya and this body of mine has the scars to prove it."

Cobs lifted the side of his shirt and showed Jack a long scar that ran the length of his ribcage. Jack could see the crude stitches that ran the length of the scar. They looked like Cobs had stitched himself up. The very thought made him wince.

"I was in the body of a Greenback Nardus, a particularly fast and tough creature, out on the slopes of Donard when a vicious Scirpus attacked me. You never want to come across one of those: every spikelet can be fatal if breathed in. It took me weeks to recover from that, even with all the healing potions at my disposal. I tried a few more times to Dream Walk but I got hurt far too often and soon I realised it wasn't worth it. When your Nanna Tess came to the InBetween all those years ago and my family and her sister never returned the day of the Great Dandelion Hunt I told her all about the Talisman. I'm not saying she stole it but soon after she left it wasn't in its secret hiding place. It had gone. I know she must have wanted desperately to find her sister Grace but I think she was too afraid ever to use it knowing she could die if anything happened to her while she was Dream Walking. Now that Tess' body has died, the Talisman is calling out to a new owner. It's calling out to you Jack."

Fearnog sat in stunned silence as his brother Cobs spoke of things he had never heard of. Only the widening of the pupils let Cobs see some hope. Cobs stared directly into Jack's eyes.

"But Jack the Talisman comes in two pieces. You must find both of them for if you sleep with the full locket, not only would you see through the eyes of whoever you inhabit you would be able to control the body as well. But you must be careful Jack, whatever happens to you whilst you Dream Walk will happen to your sleeping body so take great care. Remember you are not dreaming; you are alive in someone else's body. You must find the locket. It has to be close to you for its power to work. One last thing, as I have already said the Talisman holds great power, Tess knew this. Once you wear the Talisman, no one can take it from you for if they do it would mean their instant death. And yours…Only you can remove it"

Jack had so many questions. His mind reeled at what he had just been told but at least now he could explain his terrible fatigue and the strange new marks on his body.

All he had to do now was wake up. But how could he?

The answer came with Cobs' fast approaching fist.

Fearnog yelled out in pain.

Chapter 9

Under your nose

Jack's eyes flashed open. He rubbed his cheek from the pain of Cobs' uppercut. For such a small guy he certainly knew how to throw a punch. Jack made a mental note never to get into a scrap with him. The pain in his cheek began to subside and Jack shook his head getting his bearings. The familiar sight of the rafters overhead let him know he was back in the safety of his room. He had never been so grateful to be back in his own bed.

A single thought jumped into his head... the Talisman. Then his mind began to buzz as a million new thoughts fought one other to shout out the whereabouts of the Talisman. Jack eyes darted around his room. The wardrobe was older than he was, as were the bedside locker and chair. The only new thing that had come into the room was ancient as well and that lay beneath him. He ducked under his bed as he had done many times before and lifted out the old battered box his Nanna Tess had given him the previous year.

Somehow, the box had to be linked to his Nanna Tess' death for he never had dreams like these before she died. Whilst she had been alive the Talisman had not called out to him but it was different now. Now he knew they were not dreams at all, but Dream Walks as Cobs had called them. He had been Dream Walking. A rush of excitement filled him at the thought of what he'd been doing, not even realising the risks he'd been taking.

Up until last year, the old box lay hidden in a hollow behind a rock in the archway of the cottage. Now that Tess had passed, somehow the box was calling to him. He held it aloft but there didn't appear to be anything particularly special about it. It was what it was, just a plain old battered wooden box with a raised circular symbol carved on the top but the carvings were too worn to make out. Then Jack remembered how the raised symbol had five indentations at the edge and how they seemed to wobble when he had pressed them. He hadn't paid much heed to it then but now just maybe…

Jack placed his fingers and thumb into the five carved out indentations. When they were all in place a tiny tingle ran through his fingertips. It reminded him of touching the Silver Orb for the first time but nowhere near as painful. The faint carving began to glow white and Jack recognised the symbol as it began to take shape. It was his secret family crest, the symbol of the Elderfolk; three fish swimming in a circle. Instinctively he gave the raised symbol a twist anti-clockwise and something clicked. Jack's eyes widened as the carving on the lid came away from the box but his heart sank when he looked at the space beneath for there was nothing there, just the plain lid of the box. He quickly realised his stupidity and glanced at the underside of the piece he held in his hand. All the while he held his breath. Was this treasure about to reveal itself?

Sure enough, there it was… silver and spiky looking just like the fragile clocks on a dandelion. But what wondrous thing lay inside? It was a dazzling jewel on a fine silver chain. Jack reached into the hollowed out carving and took out the Talisman. He had never seen a diamond before but from what he'd heard he knew this glittering piece of brilliance certainly must be one. He held it up to the light and a rainbow of colours filled the room. They danced on all four walls, playing with the shadows. Jack blinked and a flash of a country hillside filled his view. He blinked again only this time he saw a winding road leading up into the mountains. He quickly realised the power of the object he held in his hand. He didn't need to be asleep to witness its power and he knew it would certainly help him on his new quest.

Now all he had to do was find the other half.

Jack put the Talisman into the wooden box and slid it back under his bed. He had a renewed vigour growing inside him. Seeing Cobs and hearing his words of encouragement gave him new hope. Together they could achieve anything. They'd already proven that.

"Jack," called Martha from inside her room. Jack didn't waste a second, he ran to her side.

"Yes Ma."

"Would you be so kind and make me something to eat? There's a dear. It's just I don't want to leave your father's side. Not for a moment."

Jack looked at his father's sunken cheeks. They were normally so full of colour but now they looked deflated as if his life had been drained from him. Then he realised, his life had been stolen from him.

"Soda bread and butter?"

"Sounds great Jack. I dunno what I'd do without ya."

Jack went to the griddle on the fire and began to make fresh soda farls. When he'd finished he looked up to

Nanna Tess' tea caddy. His Ma deserved a wee treat. He lifted out the best china pot and poured in the hot water and then he opened the tea caddy and scooped out a large spoonful of leaves. He went in for a second spoonful when he hit upon something. He fished amongst the dark leaves and lifted out a tea-stained envelope. It looked very old but with the staining from the tealeaves, it may have only looked aged. It could have been put there only a few days before but he could not tell for the letter held no date. He was about to bring it in to his mother when he noticed who it was addressed to.

Jack Turner.

Last of the Elderfolk

Jack turned the envelope over and read the words

Open only upon my death.

The handwriting was Nanna Tess'. Jack's pulse accelerated. He knew he held in his hand the answers to so many questions. He stuffed the letter into his pocket and put the caddy back on the shelf. He could hardly contain his excitement but he had to finish his chore first. He buttered the farl and brought the small meal into his mother.

"Thanks Jack," said Martha, smiling at her son.

"Do ya need anything else Ma?"

"No love, you've been more than good."

Jack didn't want to appear rude but he couldn't get out of the room quick enough.

"I'll leave you in peace then Ma."

He dashed to his room.

Chapter 10

The Letter

Jack may have only been the poor son of a fisherman but his Nanna Tess had insisted on his schooling. She sat with him every day and taught him to read and write. She explained the importance of education saying it was the one thing you could carry with no burden. It may have been difficult at first learning the alphabet and his numbers when all he wanted to do was run in the fields and play with the other children. Only now did he truly appreciate everything his Nanna had done for him. Now he held her letter in his hands staring at his name and the grand title 'Last of the Elderfolk.' Somehow, Nanna Tess knew this day would come.

Jack sat cross-legged on his bed with his back resting on the wrought iron head stead. He slipped his finger under the edge of the paper and slid it along tearing it open. Inside were pages of the most beautiful handwriting. He began to read.

To my dearest Jack,

I need to tell you my story and give you fair warning of what is ahead of you.

When I was about four years old and Grace hardly one, we were left on the steps of the local orphanage. All I know is that your great-great grandfather was called Liam and I did watch him put the stones of the archway to this cottage. He was building it for his family, my mother and my sister Grace. But we lived a fair distance away from where the cottage was. I remember us travelling all day in the cart for miles and miles and miles. It was my father Liam who told me how to make a wish on a dandelion. I just laughed.

But then I remember mother crying and saying he was gone and that I was in danger. She said she had to make sure that I was safe, safe with my sister Grace. That is why mother left us at the orphanage, to keep us safe. Safe from what I did not know.

We were taken in and given shelter in the orphanage. Finally, we were adopted by a poor man called Conor Durkin and his wife Ann, on the condition we live in the cottage. They were more than happy with the arrangement.

When I was about twelve years old everything changed. I had made a wish on a dandelion, visited the InBetween and lost Grace. Nothing could console my adopted parents and I never forgave myself for what happened.

But worse was to come. Even thinking about it now as I put pen to paper I can see her evil eyes staring at me.

There was a really old woman Jack, older than time I thought and she found me. She said she had been searching thirty lifetimes all through the world to find me and finally she sensed a powerful energy that drew her to Annalong. She told me I was not of the human realm and that I belonged to a race of Elderfolk. I didn't believe her but something in her voice told me she was not lying.

The old woman said the powerful energy she felt was a magical necklace called the Talisman of Salix. It drew her to me and put me and everyone I knew in danger. Thankfully I wasn't wearing it when we met; In fact I never wore it. I was too afraid to. She threatened me and my family if I didn't get it for her. She said she had recently killed someone to get her hands on the Talisman.

I had never been so scared in all my life Jack. I lied to her and told her I would go and get it from my house. She told me to meet her in the graveyard that evening but when I got home I was even more terrified just thinking about what had happened. I broke the Talisman in two for it came in two pieces. I placed one half of the Talisman and chain in the hollowed out section of the box and hid it behind the loose rock in the archway at the front door. The other half I hid in the bottom of my mother's special tea caddy. No one would ever think to look there for such a precious object I thought.

I stole the Talisman from Cobs' father's study but it wasn't the only thing that I took from the InBetween. I carried back all the knowledge that I had read in the Book of the Elderfolk that Cobs and I found in his study. The words I read somehow stuck inside my mind and on one of the pages was a binding spell. I placed the spell on this cottage and knew no harm could come to either me or any person who lived under its roof. I never saw that old hag again but occasionally I sensed her presence. Now that I am gone, the spell I placed on the house is broken and I am afraid she may return.

Beware Jack, the old hag is not what she seems. I cannot protect you any longer but be warned she must not get her hands on the Talisman, the Talisman is very dangerous. Keep it far from her reach. With it she has the power to change the fate of this world and all the worlds beyond...

Always remember one thing. I love you. Until we meet again, be safe.

Nanna Tess

Chapter 11

Buried Treasure

Jack could hardly believe what he'd read. He tried to make sense of everything. It was true that Tess and Grace had been orphaned but there was more to it than that. The Old Hag Doolen had lied; she didn't know Tess as a child. In fact, when she met Tess the Old Hag was already ancient. She had tried to take her Talisman when Tess was only a young girl. Bringing it back from the

InBetween somehow let Doolen track Tess down.

Jack could think no more. He jumped from his bed and ran to the fireside in the living room. There on the shelf sat the precious tea caddy. He reached up and took it down, holding it tightly in his hands. His heart seemed to beat out of sync as he dared himself to open the lid. He forced the butterflies in his stomach to calm down as he reached into the fine tea leaves. His fingers slipped through the tiny fragments of dust until he reached the bottom but he found nothing. He was sure the caddy still held a secret. Delving in for a second time he dug around in every corner of the caddy. Still there was nothing but he knew the secret was close. Jack got a dish and tipped the contents of the caddy onto it, then searched again through the leaves.

For a third time there was nothing and the frustration within Jack peaked. He picked up the caddy and shook it as hard as he could but nothing rattled as he expected. Finally he looked inside and there he saw something. At the bottom of the caddy was an elaborate circular etching and within the circle were inscribed the words of a poem. Just beneath them a tiny metal spike jutted out and it just begged to be touched. Jack held his finger over the raised piece of metal and wondered what would happen next if he pressed it. He knew Nanna Tess would have meant him no harm but it crossed his mind that it might be some sort of trap. He held his breath and winced waiting for the worst to happen. His finger hovered for a second or two and finally he pressed it.

He heard a click, but nothing more than that. There was truly nothing in the tea caddy. He slumped onto the floor annoyed with himself at building his hopes up so much. Then he heard it. A buzzing sound, a tiny buzzing sound but it grew in strength. His eyes immediately went to the metal box sitting next to him on the earthen floor. The caddy began to vibrate and bounce around the floor then it hopped into the air and floated right in front of Jack's nose. He watched in awe as the inside base of the tea caddy split and each oval section slid past the other, peeling apart to reveal a small opening and from that opening a silver flower lifted its head. At the heart of the metal blossom lay the other half of the Talisman attached to another fine silver chain.

With finger and thumb Jack carefully reached in and took it out. He looked at the glistening jewel resting in his palm. It captured the light and twinkled just like the other half he had found in the hidden lid of his wooden box.

Jack couldn't wait to unite the two pieces. But before he did he pressed the small button on the base of the tea caddy and the curved sections slid past one another until the poem revealed itself once more. This time Jack took the time to read it.

WEARER BEWARE

TWO HALVES MAKE A WHOLE

ONCE UNITED

YOU THEN SHARE A SOUL

Jack thought he understood the meaning. He remembered what Cobs had said about Salix taking over the other bodies but he never mentioned the sharing of souls. This was entirely new to him and the thought of sharing his soul scared him more than he cared to admit. He tidied up the tealeaves and placed the caddy back on the shelf. He didn't want anyone finding the evidence. Then he went back to his room and got the other half of the Talisman and chain from its resting place. Jack held one-half in his palm and the other in his fingers. Slowly he united the two pieces and a piercing light exploded out in all directions. Jack shielded his eyes until the light finally dimmed. The Talisman glowed gently now from within and from time to time, it sparkled like the summer sun on a flowing river. Jack thought of Grace's tears held in the tiny bottle. Could they be one and the same?

With the Talisman of Salix pieced together Jack was about to hang it around his neck but he stopped. Something that Nanna Tess had written in his letter sprang to mind; the warning. He placed the necklace in the battered box and ran to Tess' bedroom. Everything was as she had left it. Jack knew where she kept her precious belongings. He had seen her putting them there one night as he passed her room and the door was ajar. He opened her wardrobe and lifted out the small bundle of papers tucked in under the blankets.

The letters were all written by Tess and when Jack removed the fine cord that bound them together they slipped onto the bed in a small heap. He opened the first one and quickly realised they were not letters. They didn't have exactly the same handwriting as the letter he found in the tea caddy. This writing looked ancient. Like the Ogham symbols he saw back in the InBetween when he found the family Hawksbeard. But it wasn't Ogham, it looked even older. If Jack didn't know any better he would have said that these were not letters. They looked more like spells. Magic spells. Down the sides of the pages were lists of ingredients, on one Jack could see a sketch of his cottage with a bubble around it. Could that have been what Tess was telling him about?

On the third page of Tess' writings, Jack came across a sketch of the Talisman. It showed a man standing tall wearing the chain but back to front. It showed another man lying on the ground, possibly dead with the necklace with the Talisman on his chest. He breathed a sigh of relief knowing he could have come so close to his own demise.

The rest of the pages depicted strange objects and designs. He could make no sense at all of them except one. It showed a tree in a tree that Jack knew to be the Curraghard Tree but looming over it was a cloud of darkness and a cloud of light. He didn't feel easy looking at it so he closed all the papers except for the one he needed about the Talisman and put them back where he had found them.

Jack went back to his room, opened the box, took out the two united Talismans, and held it in his hands. He breathed in deeply as he slipped both chains over his head, careful to follow the instructions on the page in front of him, making sure the Talisman rested on the back of his neck. He then stuffed the sheet of paper into his trouser pocket.

Choosing to leave your body to travel into another creature is something most people could not contemplate. Choosing to share your soul is even more unimaginable. What would drive a boy to do such a thing? Why would someone give up the safety of their own home no matter what the cost?

But Jack Turner was no ordinary boy; he had fought a battle with no weapons. It was he who had found pathways that never existed but now he was about to embark on a journey that meant life or death.

He crossed his fingers on both hands and closed his eyes.

Chapter 12

Dream Walker

Summer in Tollymore Forest is better than your mind's eye can conjure. The River Shimna sparkles diamond-like as it cascades over smooth granite rocks and plunges down great heights in magnificent waterfalls under the canopy of green leafy trees and between the azaleas in full blossom on the river banks. The cackle, caw and chirp of many birds merge with the buzz of a million insects and every corner and dark crevice of the forest bustles with life.

But this time when Jack arrived in the forest he noticed something different, something very different. He noticed something... missing. He had arrived at the same old ruin amongst the trees, the same ruin that the stones from the archway in his cottage were made from. He had arrived in a different form, a different body this time. This time Jack stood no taller than a toadstool and it took him a second to get used to his new perspective. His eyesight was sharper than ever he could have imagined. It was comparable to being in the peregrine falcon again, but that time he had thought it only a dream, now he knew better. He also was fully aware of the dangers attached. He looked at two tiny paws stretched out in front of him and he looked over his furry shoulder at a huge red bushy tail. He giggled out loud and a chattering sound came out past his two tiny buck teeth.

He surveyed the Shimna River in front of him. The first thing he noticed amongst all the splendour and beauty of the forest were the stepping-stones. He noticed them because... they were not there. The very stones that had saved him from the Drinns had vanished. He wondered if they would ever reappear. Who knew where they had gone?

Jack scurried along the banks of the Shimna River hopping over twisted tree roots that reached up through the dark soil and dodged nettles and jagged holly bushes until he came across a small rickety wooden bridge. He had no fear it would hold his weight for he knew a squirrel weighed a lot less than a boy. Again he heard a chatter pass his buck teeth as he bounced from beam to beam until he came to the other side. There was only one destination in mind but the tiny body Jack occupied would take some time to get there. Undeterred he carried on; a squirrel can cover a lot of ground in a day if it puts its mind to it.

A small boy lay sleeping on his bed. His eyes darted from one side of their sockets to the other but his eyelids remained firmly shut. All the while another set of eyes watched him. The other eyes were pearls of darkness looking at Jack from beyond the walls of his cottage. They were the eyes of an ancient hag biding her time. She knew the moment to pounce and she waited with baited breath.

Scurry, scurry, and hop. Hop, duck, scurry, leap. The first branch reached. Hop, hop Leap. Another branch reached. Run, run, spring. The third branch reached and so it continued until the tiny squirrel had scaled the heights of the Curraghard Tree. He reached the Hawksbeard's mansion perched precariously on the inner tree. The mansion shored up on straining beams of wood and good luck.

Tap, tap, tap. The tiny paws rapped on the mosaic glass of an ornate window frame.

Wait, wait, wait…. No reply. The tiny heart nestled in the squirrel's rib cage beat faster than Jack thought possible. He remembered another way and scampered along an especially long branch until it found a small window half-open. He squeezed through the gap, entered the room and marvelled at the familiar sight of the hearth, blazing fire and mantle piece with the eleven hollowed out silver spoons nailed to it.

The squirrel found a crumpled up old bunch of papers on the old bureau in the corner of the room and he nestled into them and waited. After an hour being hypnotised by purple sparks from fire shooting up the chimney he heard the door of the study click open. Someone entered. He wore a crooked hat, a multicoloured patchwork waistcoat. He didn't look like the happiest Clurichaun in all the land considering he had just been reunited with his family. There should have been a smile running from pointed ear to pointed ear but instead thin pursed lips stood in their place.

Cobs stood resplendent in his new clothes. The shabby traveller he once was could not be mistaken for the new prince of the Kingdom of Mourne. But why did he look so troubled?

The squirrel took its chance, leapt from the mantelpiece and landed on Cobs' forearm. Cobs had no time to react before he was staring into the eyes of a close fiend.

"Jack. It's you!"

The squirrel held up two paws and tilted its head to one side. Cobs recognised the sarcasm in the gesture immediately. It may only have been a squirrel but Cobs knew an old friend when he saw one.

"Those eyes are all too familiar Jack but such a host is not becoming of a young man of your importance. Now come on, quickly."

Cobs carried the tiny creature over to his father's bureau and whispered into his ear.

"The dwellers of the InBetween and the Inner Realm have come to a truce. Now that the Silver Orb has been shattered, thanks to you, the Inner Realm no longer exists and my father Poitin and the Dullahan are forging a treaty of trust and understanding. They will hold council and both will agree that peace must be preserved at all costs. The treaty will be held under lock and key and no one may look upon it"

Cobs began to frown. Jack could clearly see this and his tiny heart began to beat even faster.

"I know I should be rejoicing right now but there's only one problem Jack… something doesn't feel quite right. All the creatures of the Inner Realm have been set free and all the creatures of the InBetween were free to welcome them but still there seems to be something unsettling, something that doesn't want the realms to get along."

Cobs was about to continue but the door of the study suddenly flew open and the children of the

Hawksbeard clan fell into the room, along with many of the creatures from the Inner Realm. They were laughing, dancing and tripping over one another. The family festivities had only just begun. They had been apart for so long that they had to celebrate; the Orb had been broken and many more creatures walked in the InBetween. It was certainly something to be grateful for and celebrate. These creatures, evil and twisted had learned that the only way to live was to get along, to understand their differences, and learn to tolerate one another. A Pookah may not see eye to eye with a Merrow, a changeling may never agree with a Sheerie but that did not mean they couldn't share the same piece of land with respect and understanding. Now that land included all of the Mourne Mountains.

Jack could see the merriment from inside one of the tiny half-open drawers that was full to overflowing with maps and trinkets from the hills. Now that the Shimnavore had been defeated and everything had a proper order, Jack knew there was a lot to prepare; days of feasting, mead to be gathered in Poitin's barrels. But what Cobs had said troubled him. He knew something was very wrong in his world but he truly believed that smashing the Silver Orb was the right thing to do. Now he didn't seem so certain. Was there a link to what happened to his father and the feeling Cobs described?

Cobs stood with his back to Jack, concealing him, and coughed aloud trying to get everyone in the room's attention. No one listened. He raised his voice; still no one paid him any heed. He put an index finger to each side of his lips and let out an ear-screeching whistle that could only have been taught to him by a Sheerie. The room fell silent.

"I know we all have reason to celebrate but might I ask all of you to leave the room. All of you that is, except for my brothers and sister. I promise it won't be long but I need to ask them something very important."

There were a few disgruntled sighs as the Inner Realm inhabitants left the room. The door closed behind them.

"I'm so sorry I had to do that. Will everyone be seated I have something I need to discuss."

Each member of the family found somewhere to sit. Trom sat cross legged on the floor and placed his hands on his knees drumming his fingers as he always did, much to the annoyance of the others. Malip and Cran Cno took the over-stuffed sofa, with Fearnog and Coll sitting on the arms. Cuileann, Iur and Beith sat on the hearth, the fire warming their backs.

Fearnog was the first to stand. He had skin weathered to the colour of Irish Mahogany, an oval face with a neatly trimmed grey beard and long curls that fell from his sideburns like catkins. His waistcoat, for every Clurichaun wore one, was of mauve squares of all shades with fine cracked vertical lines running through them. He was tall for a Clurichaun, standing only half an inch shorter than his father Poitin.

"Is something wrong brother? I am in need of a drink. I am as dry as the Trassey Track on a hot summer's day. I would have thought of all people you would have had reason to rejoice."

"I agree," said Beith standing up. It was tradition in the family that when they called a family meeting the one who spoke would stand. It saved a lot of in-fighting that way. "What on this side of Hare's Gap could be troubling you?" Beith was the pioneer in the family, always the first at everything. It may have had something to do with the fact that she was the only girl. The rest of them never made allowances for that. They were all equal in their parent's eyes. Beith could hold her own and defend herself but she had the purest of spirit that matched her beauty. Her Da said she could drive the Devil out of the wickedest of hearts. She toyed with her fair hair as she spoke. It fell in long flowing braids all the way past her slate grey waistcoat with its sprigs of bright green all the way through it. Her edge of her dress met her shiny boots in gold brocade.

Cobs was a little surprised that she hadn't been the first to speak. He began to pace up and down the room with his hands held behind his back. He cleared his throat.

"None of you will ever know the happiness I feel for getting you all back and I dearly hope none of you ever feel the loneliness of the one hundred years without you. But there is something I must tell you. I have had the strangest feeling since Jack Turner left our realm, a bad feeling. Now my instincts have just proven justified. Jack Turner is in mortal danger. Now I must ask one of you to put their lives in danger. But which one of you?"

"But how could you know that?" asked Iur leaping to his feet.

"I have had a visit from a Dream Walker," replied Cobs.

Everyone gathered gasped in horror.

Chapter 13

Family

This is a brief interruption from the Author.

Now might not be the best time but I thought maybe the rest of the family should be properly introduced. If you don't want to know more about them you can skip straight to the next chapter to see what Cobs is going to say but you will miss out on some amazing facts about the Hawksbeard clan. Each member of the family has powers and strengths and I will even reveal their weaknesses.

There are so many of them and their names are quite unusual but once you see where they came from you might understand better. You have already met Fearnog and Beith and Iur was just about to shove his tuppence worth in.

To refresh your memories Cobs has seven brothers and one sister. There's Fearnog, Beith, Iur, Cran Cno, Malip, Cuileann, Coll and Trom. They range in ages but were born within a couple of centuries of each other, give or take a couple of decades. They are a great bunch of people and like any ordinary family they quarrel and fight. Mind you they aren't like and ordinary family. None that I am aware of anyway. Never have I met so many children with the same parents to have so many different skin colours, hair colours and eye colours. Poitin called them all his rainbow of joy and they all seemed to like that. So I shall begin to tell you just a little bit about each of them for one of them is about to step into the breach and do something incredibly brave. Now I don't know about you but when someone does something nice for me I like to know a little bit about them. But then again maybe I'm just nosey that way.

Oh and by the way I will not interrupt the book again before it is finished. At least, I don't think I will. I can be quite fickle sometimes too. I change my mind in the same way the wind changes direction. Anyhow let me begin to tell you about Cob's family.

Fearnog and Beith have already been mentioned but a little bit more about their background wouldn't do any harm. I will list them in order of birth starting with the eldest.

Fearnog

Fearnog is the eldest of the family and asserts this fact whenever he can. He has the ability to project a false image of himself (like a doppelganger). He repels water like a duck. It is said the saying 'water off a duck's back' refers to Fearnog but who am I to say if that is true. He can cut through water and swim faster than any Watershee. But because of his power he can find it hard to wash and sometimes can whiff a bit and he has to drink a lot of water to stay alive. He is a master dandelion hunter with the greatest record ever for making children's wishes come true. His favourite pastimes are bog snorkelling and bouldering.

Trom

Trom is a rather untidy Clurichaun and has a fiery heart when this is brought up. His clothes are shabby, especially his purple waistcoat. There are more purple patches on it and there is a great doubt that any of the original waistcoat still exists. He is rather small even for a Clurichaun and is often seen tiptoeing around the house. He says it is to make sure he doesn't disturb anyone but everyone knows the real reason. He is another Clurichaun with grey white hair making him look older than he really is. He has the reddest cheeks of anyone you have ever seen and in late summer, they are nearly the colour of ripe strawberries. He wears a massive unruly beard and would nearly give him the look of a bear or goat. Trom has a very protective nature and prefers the company of others. He has an unusual body odour that whilst not unpleasant can make you drowsy. He makes the most amazing tea in the entire world and enjoys nothing more than sharing a cup and telling others all the tales about humans. No one knows more about humans than Trom.

Cuileann

Cuileann has the happiest disposition of any creature ever to walk the land. He has rather a prickly nature though with a deep understanding of the darker side of life. He has the amazing ability to shrink himself down to the size of a.... well put it this way, when he shrinks you cannot see him so I don't know how small that is but dust comes to mind. He is also quite the person to have around in a storm for he can control lightning given the right circumstances. This is a feat the other Hawksbeards have witnessed and hold this in high regard. Cuileann has the smoothest and palest of complexions, even Beith is envious. Cuileann can be easily offended but he never holds grudges. His family waistcoat is rosy red but made from very very scratchy wool.

Malip

Malip has a rebellious, tough streak running through him. He has been known to argue for hours on the fact that black might very well be white. When he's in that kind of mood the rest are known to scarper. He loves to be out and about with other people of like mind. He likes the company of the grumpy Stoney Riggs. They are a monotonous race of stone shape shifters and have been around forever. They delight in argument and long monologs about the meaning of life. They can talk for days on the merits of blue mould. Anyway, back to Malip. Malip is a handsome Clurichaun. Some would say very dashing. He has rough rugged features and many a female Clurichaun have been swayed by his charms. He is strong, hardy and can endure the harsh mountains even though he has a tall thin frame. He can take a knock and not even know it. His favourite place is at the foothills of Slieve Donard where a certain Lady Clurichaun called Calluneta is believed to live. He is never seen without his waistcoat of bright orange with red and green diamond shapes running throughout in a random but never in a clashing manner. The strangest thing about Malip is that he carries a set of golden keys with him at all times. He says they're important but he hasn't a clue what doors they might open. In his spare time he likes to yodel and play the fiddle.

Coll

Coll is the tallest of nearly all the Clurichauns. He has an immediate presence when he enters a room. Not because of his height, he has let us say a very wide base also, all right for those who didn't get the hint, he's fat. A rough complexion with a well trimmed beard would nearly give the impression of an aristocrat. But the strange thing is every year in and around April his beard falls off in one piece like leaves of a well shaken tree. Coll is an avid bird watcher but equally loves all the animals of the forest. He keeps a pet dormouse in the left hand pocket of his waistcoat that is bright yellow and has green circular patches. The dormouse isn't that colour I hope you realise, he's plain brown. Coll's great size equals his immense strength. But he has a gentle soul and has a poetic nature. He carries a hazel staff shaped like a shepherd's crook with him at all times. The one problem with Coll is that he is very susceptible to the dreaded BLOTCH. This is a disease once dreaded by Clurichauns and Leprechauns alike for it spreads like wild fire and causes an itch that cannot be relieved with scratch or barbed wire. The cure was simple though and Poitin found it many moons ago. A quick dip in the River Shimna on a day when there is a sun and moon in the sky.

That could be a long wait when you have an itch.

Cran Cno

Cran Cno is an average Clurichaun. He is of medium build and height but has a great posture, always standing tall and proud and it makes him look taller than he really is. He has yellowish brown skin and dark dark hair on top of a constantly furrowed brow. He's best described as a worry-wort. His sharply pointed teeth with their large gaps can be a bit off putting when he smiles because it gives him an air of menace but nothing could be further from the truth. Cran Cno adores the winter for he likes nothing more than the freezing cold outdoors. It is said, by those lucky enough to have witnessed it, that he has the power over insects and other minute creatures. What use this might be I cannot fathom but an unusual gift none the less. But I have heard he is friends with the coldest insects of all, the Spicicles; the Spiders of Ice. A rare breed and soon to be extinct. They are dying out but no one knows why. Cran Cno is great with his hands and builds many a tree house dwelling for other Clurichauns. He is a master shoemaker and can make anything from leather. Oh and his waistcoat is bright gold with a hint of icy blue running in faint squares lines throughout.

Iur

Iur is wise beyond his years. He was the first child to talk even without the potion to help understanding. He is quiet for a Clurichaun, almost mystical or spiritual in nature. He has the remarkable power of recuperation, meaning he heals remarkably quickly. He just places his hand into the soil and whatever his ailment it is soon gone. He says he communes with nature but no one else really understands what he means but they are jealous nonetheless. He can also spread his healing powers to others and has been known to bring people back from the brink. It might be something to do with the fact that he is the seventh son. Whether Poitin is also the seventh son I do not know. Iur doesn't dress like your average Clurichaun, preferring robes when out on the hills. But he does wear a waistcoat under them. It is the most colourful also with purples and hues of green and yellow. He wears tall lopsided hats of copper. His worst trait is his temper. And best to stay well away from him in a full moon.

Beith

Beith is a mechanical wizard. She delights in making toys for all her family and friends. Her masterpiece was a present given to Pierce for his castle ballroom. It was two ballroom dancers, perfect in every detail; an exact copy of her parents and Pierce brings them out on every Summer Solstice Ball. Her only flaw is her trusting nature, always seeing the best in people.

And finally Cobs. But what more can be said of Cobs? He is honourable, charming and the best friend a young human could ever hope to have.

Now we can get on with the story.

So there is no confusion the next chapter will be called Chapter 13 in case you skipped this chapter and left off at chapter 12. If you did read this chapter and I am glad you did then you can call the next chapter 14 but only in your head so you don't get to confused.

Now where were we? Oh yes...

We left off with Cobs about to ask an important question and telling everyone about the Dream Walker. They are still in shock.

Chapter 13

Short straw

Cobs continued to pace up and down the room looking at the shocked faces of his siblings.

"I thought that was a story we were told as children to make sure we behaved," said Trom rocking back and forward as he was given to when he was scared or annoyed.He stood up and gave his neck a massive crack. Everyone winced, they hated when he cricked his neck. It sounded gross and everyone rolled their shoulders. The shoulder rolling spread through the room like a yawn.

"Same here Trom," interrupted Malip. "I remember the tale. If you don't be good the Dream Walker will come, he will find you and he will take over your body. Then you'll have no choice but to be good. I had nightmares about that for years. Now you're trying to say there is actually some truth in it Cobs?"

Cobs stopped dead and turned to his family. "Not only do I know it to be true. I have proof in this very room."

The room erupted in nervous chatter. Beith gripped the arm of her brother and he grabbed her back just as hard.

"And now to introduce you to the Dream Walker." Cobs went over to the bureau and put his arm out straight.

But there was no one there. He rummaged in the pile of papers he had seen Jack in earlier but now he was gone.

Jack was fighting the urge to bolt. He had the oddest craving for nuts and berries and if he didn't get them soon he was sure he was going to explode. 'Berries, berries, berries. Must have berries. Maybe some nuts, yeah nuts will do just fine. I know where to get some lovely pine nuts...'

"Where are you ya little varmint?" called Cobs.

Jack heard his friend's voice and he snapped out of his trace-like desire for all things gobblingly delicious for a squirrel. He skirted up the curtain, along the pole and back onto the the old bureau. He leapt onto Cobs' leather arm gauntlet and sat straight upright with his tiny ginger hairy arms outstretched as if to say, 'TA DA...'

"You mean to tell me I've been having nightmares about a squirrel?" shouted Malip. Jack's tiny eyes watched as Malip burst into a fit of uncontrollable laughter. It was surely infectious for within a few seconds the laughter had spread to everyone. They were holding their sides rolling on the floor.

"Good one Cobs, we always knew you liked a prank but a Dream Walking Squirrel has to take the biscuit. How did you come up with that?" asked Fearnog, clearly enjoying the joke.

Cobs just stood waiting for the rabble to calm down. He looked directly into Jack's eyes who just shrugged his squirrelly shoulders.

"I know Jack, just you wait to see what happens when they realise the truth." Cobs stomped his foot onto the floorboards trying to restore some order but it had the opposite effect. The siblings rolled around even more. After a good five minutes only a snigger or two could only be heard. Cobs continued to stand in one spot holding the tiny squirrel on his arm and soon Jack could see realisation spread across one or two of their faces.

"You're not joking are you Cobs?" said Cran Cno.

Cobs just shook his head. "I've never been more serious and when you've all quite finished we need to talk. "

Everyone took their seats again and Cobs continued.

"Believe it or not this little furry friend here is Jack Turner. He has found the Talisman of Salix and now has the power to live inside the body of another. That is why I have called you all together. There is no way we can let this young man suffer alone. We must find out why he desperately needs our help. That is why I need your cooperation."

"You have our undivided attention brother," said Iur. He stared harshly at the others in case he heard a snigger or saw a sarcastic grin.

"Thank you. Jack Turner needs something that only one of you can give. I would not trust this with any one else. It is much too serious to tell Mother or Father. They would forbid it."

"Will you spit it out Cobs for goodness sake? There's no need to go up the Cooley Mountains and down the Fairy Glen," said Beith.

Cobs glanced at Jack's eyes and then into the eyes of each one of his kin.

"This young man needs a body to live in."

Utter pandemonium ensued. Jack watched as brother argued with brother. He was quite frightened when blows were nearly exchanged as the arguing became heated. All Cobs could think about was that they would have to draw straws and the one who pulled the short straw would have no choice.

"It is to be my duty," screamed Beith.

"Certainly not, you are a mere…" Malip was interrupted by a swift kick in the rear end.

"Don't you dare say it is because I am a girl," hissed Beith.

Her face had turned scarlet from anger and so had Malip's but his red face was from the indignity of being kicked up the rear-end.

"I wasn't going to say anything of the sort. I was going to say a mere mechanical wizard. This needs to be … never mind" said Malip.

As Cobs and Jack watched the commotion unfold, the heated argument of Malip and Beith, Trom and Cuileann, Cran Cno and Iur, they soon began to realize that the Hawksbeards were not trying to shy away from their duty, quite the contrary; they were fighting for the honour to help Jack Turner.

"Hold on, hold on everyone. I cannot believe how brave you all are and I am delighted to have you as my family."

Everyone stopped to listen to what Cobs had to say.

"We will draw straws."

All the Hawksbeards agreed that it was the only way. Jack went over to the fire, lifted the small hearth brush, and plucked eight pieces of straw from it. He broke one in half and then placed them all in his hand. They all looked the same length and only when picked would the short straw be revealed.

Cobs held out his hand and everyone picked a straw. Malip stopped and looked the squirrel straight into his eyes.

"I hope it's me Jack." And he tickled him under his tiny furry chin.

Jack smiled a squirrelly smile and all the while thought of nuts and berries, nuts and berries, actually no... berries and nuts and maybe a toadstool, one of those red and white spotty ones that his mother always said were poisonous to humans.

When all the straws had been picked, everyone compared what they held in their hands. Trom had drawn the short straw. Somehow winning didn't seem so great now. He thought the odds were so good that the chances of picking him were a long shot. It wasn't that he was a coward, it was just the unsettling thought of what was about to happen. But a bargain was a bargain and he would not show his fear and let Cobs or Jack down.

Cobs sat on the chair at the bureau and began talking to Jack. He explained that he needed all the energy he could muster to leap into Trom and only by staring into each other's eyes whilst thinking of the same thing would it be possible. If not done correctly one of them could be lost forever. The squirrel made a tiny gulp but Trom's could be heard throughout the room. No one said anything for they all were aware how serious a matter this was.

"Could everyone except Trom leave the room now? I will call you when it's all over. And for goodness sake don't let mother or father find out."

Each one of the Hawksbeards left the room after shaking the tiny squirrel paw, wishing it luck, and patting Trom on his shoulder.

When a quiet hush descended on the study Cobs lifted the squirrel over to Trom and placed him on his arm. They stared at one another.

"Now," said Cobs, "What you are about to do is very dangerous. I have only read about it in father's book when I had all that time on my hands waiting for your return. I couldn't fully understand all what he wrote but there were enough wee sketches to fill in the blanks."

The squirrel let out a tiny squeak and so did Trom for that matter. Neither of them could see a middle finger and an index finger twist over one another as Cobs crossed them for luck.

"Now I want you both to think of the River Shimna. Think of the summer sunrays pouring through the overlying trees and playing with the ebbs and eddies of the water below. Think of how calm this makes you both feel. Think of how warm you feel inside. Nothing can harm you. You are becoming part of the river. You are becoming part of the water. Jack you are flowing and Trom you are flowing. You are flowing past one another and into one another."

The two willing participants were staring into each other's eyes; squirrel into Clurichaun's and Clurichaun into squirrel's.

"Now Jack," Cobs said calmly, "I want you to concentrate on Trom's eyes. Look at those dark cat-like irises. Now look beyond that, look into his pupils. Look at the darkness of those pupils. Think of the River Shimna, think of those pupils. You are drowning in those pupils but you feel safe. You must become one with them. Now close your eyes."

Both the squirrel and Trom closed their eyes and they waited. After a few moments, Trom's eyes shot open and he let out a yelp. Cobs could instantly see that the eyes of his brother Trom had become Jack Turner's eyes.

"We did it Jack, we did it."

Just as Cobs was about to jump for joy and give Jack a great big hug the study door burst open again but this time Cob's father Poitin entered.

"Oi Cobs, Trom, everyone has gathered in the great dining hall, hurry up. I wondered where you two got to."

Trom, who was now controlled by Jack, looked away so Poitin couldn't see his eyes and know something had happened to him.

"We'll be out now Father," said Cobs. "Jack is just..." Cobs stopped himself mid-sentence very flustered and red faced, "I mean Trom was just asking me what I got up to while you all slept for a hundred years."

Poitin rested his hands on his large belly and laughed heartily. The golden buttons on his bright red waistcoat strained under the excess pressure his merriment had caused.

"Alright now, but don't be too long. The Dullahan wants to show everyone a trick. He is carving a giant pumpkin as we speak and has your mother fetching him a candle."

Poitin left the study and the secret door shut behind him leaving only a wall of books. Cobs couldn't help but notice Trim fidgeting uncontrollably.

"Are   you   all   right?"
"Of course I am Cobs," said Jack but with Trom's voice. "But I was trying to hold on to this poor wee critter. As soon as I jumped into Trom's body the squirrel became himself again and bit right into my finger. Why do ya think I jumped up as I did? The fight was nearly more than I could take," said Jack taking the struggling squirrel over to the window and happily releasing it.

"Now Jack," said Cobs." You must tell me everything."

To make it easier for everyone from now on Trom will be called Jack. But remember anyone looking at Jack will only see Trom. So there might be occasions when the name Trom will be used. It'll keep you on your toes and remember Trom is often on tip toe anyway.

Chapter 14

Now what?

"When I returned home from the InBetween and went into my Nanna Tess' room. I must have been the happiest boy in any realm you could ever imagine. The woman who helped raise me was waiting in bed but what she told me shocked me beyond belief. She told me she had met you a very long time ago and how Grace got lost with everyone else."

Cobs looked guilty hearing his friend speak and Jack could see this.

"Don't worry Cobs. I know it wasn't your fault, just a silly prank. If anything you saved Tess' life. If it weren't for you Tess would have been with all the others..."

Cobs smiled a little. Jack could see he had never considered this before and some of the guilt lifted from his shoulders.

"But Cobs, Tess told me the most amazing of all things."

"What Jack?"

"That I'm the last of the Elderfolk."

"What? " said Cobs. He stood dumbfounded at the revelation.

"But how do you know this?" said Cobs. His cat-like pupils widened.

"Nanna Tess told me. I don't know how she knew Cobs and I didn't stop to ask. I was too excited about possibly seeing my father again that I ran out of Nanna Tess' bedroom. By the time I got back..."

Jack told Cobs about how upset he had been finding his Nanna Tess when he'd returned from the pier with his mother. He explained in detail his utter delight mixed with abject horror at his father's return and the three words he spoke. But most frightening of all was the appearance of the Old Hag Doolen. Cobs listened intently and spoke in a way only true friends can speak to one another; with kindness, humility and real understanding. He reassured Jack that now he knew about his father's peril he would do everything to help.

Cobs didn't dwell on the fact that he too sensed something was very wrong going on in the InBetween and somehow their two dilemmas were linked.

"This is incredible. You are a descendent of the Elderfolk. I knew you had a secret inside you but I never dreamed it was this. I wonder how you are linked to them, after all you are human and they... well... let's just say they weren't from this realm, or yours for that matter Jack."

Jack beamed with pride. His new family secret felt great to share.

"No one else can know Jack. It could put you in grave danger. Do you understand?"

Jack nodded but an image of Nanna Tess flashed into his mind and his smile dropped, replaced with a frown. Cobs immediately could tell his friend was in need of cheering up.

"Before we begin the next part of our quest together Jack, there is one thing I must show you. It will lift your spirits and fill your heart with such joy nothing will discourage you until we find what we seek. Come with me"

Cobs took Jack by the arm and he led him through the maze of beautiful corridors of the house. Cobs pointed out many artefacts along the way and where they had come from, some not entirely honest either but 'all's fair game to a roving Cluricahun' said Cobs in passing. Together they made their way to the vast dining hall.

The feast had begun.

Plucked harp strings fought to be heard over the bowing of the fiddles and the stamping of shod boots. At the head of the long oak dining table with a giant pumpkin for a head sat the Dullahan, a carved smile from one side of the great orange ball to the other under two glowing candle-lit eyes.

The scene was nothing short of remarkable. Pookah danced with Merrow, Clurichaun skipped with Changeling, a Sheerie was arm in arm with a banshee spinning around for all they were worth. Each and every Clurichaun was linking arm in arm in a circle and running in and out, laughing as they went.

"This truly is heart-warming Cobs, just as you said it would be."

But Cobs just shook his head knowingly. He couldn't hear a word Jack had just said over the noise. He led Jack around the edge of the bustling crowd. Then he stopped and pointed into the adjoining room where two young girls sat, deep in conversation. One wore a red dress, the other a cream with a pink ribbon around her waist.

"I just wanted to show you someone."

Jack looked where Cobs had indicated and he could see two young girls sitting together totally engrossed in conversation. Jack thought he recognised one of them. Then it dawned on him...the girl on the cliffside; the girl who gave him the Obsidian Stone. That meant...

Cobs could see Jack piecing it all together.

Jack was just about to cry out to them but Cobs put his hand over Jack's mouth and stopped him. It was slightly quieter where they now stood and Cobs could just about be heard.

"Yes Jack that is Tess." He let it sink in for a moment. It was one thing thinking you knew something but entirely another having it confirmed. "And that younger girl with her is Grace."

Jack was about to run over to them and throw his arms about them and hug them and scream with all the joy he felt in his heart but Cobs caught his arm.

"Hold on a moment Jack. They look so happy to be reunited, don't you think that we should let them be for now don't you?"

"What. Are you mad? That's my Nanna Tess sitting there and my long lost great Aunt Grace. No Cobs I won't hold on for a moment. For another thing Tess has answers for me Cobs. She knows all about the letter she wrote, all about Elderfolk and the Old Hag. She might be able to help with getting my father's soul back safely. I have got to talk to her."

"I'm afraid it isn't as simple as that Jack." Cobs held Jack firmly by the wrist now and planted his tiny feet firmly on the ground. "Yes that is your Nanna Tess sitting over there. No one but my father, mother and I know who she is. When I saw her with Grace in her embrace I knew immediately who she was, even with her youthful appearance, then I realised she could only be here given one fact... the fact that she must be a descendent of the Elderfolk and therefore Grace too. I don't know how, but it all fell into place. But Tess has only arrived here from the Outer Realm. Her memories will not have fully formed yet. As far as she is aware she has just arrived for the first time and is with her sister Grace. Her memories will come back as I say but if you go to her now all you will do to the poor wee thing is scare her and I'm sure you don't want that?"

"But back there a few minutes ago you looked surprised when I told you I was one of the Elderfolk. You already knew. Why didn't you say anything?"

"And steal your thunder. What did you expect me to say? Oh yeah, sure I know that. Can you imagine how you would have felt? I could see the pride oozing from every pore in your body. No. Everyone needs their moment in the sun. There is an old saying Jack 'Melodious is the closed tongue.'"

Jack laughed at the saying and he reluctantly agreed with what Cobs had just told him. All he wanted to do was throw his arms around his Nanna Tess and tell her everything. But she wouldn't understand because of her memory and it wouldn't have helped matters that he was in Trom's body. Jack decided it was best to watch the party and his Nanna Tess and Grace from afar.

A voice from the centre of the room called out. It was Poitin.

"I hereby call upon the best singer in the room to come forward and regale us with the Hawksbeard family song. It was written many, many full moons ago tells of how we came to be here and how long we have left on this earth. It tells of ancient beings and descendants, of foes and friends."

Jack looked around the room to see who was being called upon and he began to notice that more and more eyes were falling upon him. He immediately glanced at Cobs who was blushing crimson.

"I don't think it fair father," said Cobs.

"Nonsense boy. Sure Trom could charm the skin of a Searon with that voice and that's no mean feat considering a Searon hasn't got any ears."

The room burst into laughter followed by the clapping of hands to encourage Trom to take centre stage.

"I'm afraid you've no choice Jack... I mean Trom," said Cobs.

"What father says goes."

Jack kept his head bowed and he tipped his flat hat further forward to cover his eyes. As he moved to take the middle of the stage he mouthed to Cobs that he didn't know the words of the Hawksbeard family song and it wasn't likely he would learn them in the next fifteen seconds. The room was cheering so loudly the very walls and floors were vibrating. Jack cleared his throat and from under his hat scanned all those gathered. He couldn't afford to be found out. Too much was depending on him.

He had to save his father. That was it... His father. His father was the answer. Jack imagined he was standing with his father and his friend John Connolly who had taught him the song.

He cleared his throat and began.

"As I roved by the dockside one evening so fair
To view the salt waters and take in the salt air
I heard an old fisherman singing this song
Oh, take me away boys me time is not long

Dress me up in me oilskin and blankets
No more on the docks I'll be seen
Just tell me old shipmates, I'm taking a trip mates
And I'll see you someday on Fiddlers Green

Now Fiddlers' Green is a place I've heard tell
Where the fishermen go if they don't go to hell
Where the weather is fair and the dolphins do play
And the cold coast of Greenland is far, far away

Now when you're in dock and the long trip is
through
There's pubs and there's clubs and there's lassies
there too
And the girls are all pretty and the beer is all free
And there's bottles of rum growing on every tree.

Now the skies always clear and there's never a gale
And the fish jump on board with one swish on their
tail
Where you lie at your leisure, there's no work to do
And the skipper's below making tea for the crew

Now I don't want a harp nor a halo, not me
Just give me a breeze and a good rolling sea
I'll play me old squeeze-box as we sail along
With the wind in the riggin' to sing me a song."

Jack stopped singing but the room remained silent. Whilst he sang no one drew breath. They had never heard anything quite like it; it mesmerized and frightened them in equal measure. Trom seemed different to them but they couldn't quite put their finger on it. Cobs began a slow clap and soon everyone joined in and thanked Jack (or Trom as they knew him). He took a bow and left the raised platform, sweat streaming down his face. His nerves could hold out no longer.

"You played a blinder there Jack," said Cobs. "No one was any the wiser."

"You listen to me you fart from a Drareg's Butts. Never, ever do anything like that to me again, you hear me?" And Jack stormed off with clenched fists pressed firmly to his sides.

Cobs stood in stunned silence. There was no way Jack knew about Draregs, let alone them having two butts, and only Trom could have come up with such an excellent insult. Sibling rivalry runs deep in most children but these siblings remained young for many centuries so they could appear even crueler to each other.

Games were played, ancient tales told and songs of long forgotten heroes were brought back to life with a renewed vigour. The gifts bestowed to new friends were plenty and varied. What in the world a banshee would do with a new comb she couldn't think but she thanked Beith none the less. The Changeling delighted in his new shoes Cran Cno had made that stretched magically when he changed from innocent infant to a decrepit twisted creature. To carry on with listing the presents would be both exhausting and after a while tiresome, suffice to say that all were happy beyond belief. The two best friends, who quickly made up after Jack's outburst, sat and watched everything going on for they knew a night of reverie would harm no one.

The sun rose on the Curraghard Tree and filled its corners with warmth and light. Every room was full to bursting with slumbering guests. Trom snored so loudly Cobs was suddenly woken. He shook his brother who gruffly replied with a sharp elbow and a 'leave me alone.' Cobs knew instantly that Jack had left his brother's body, as he slept, and had returned to his own. It was most important that Jack looked after himself in the Outer Realm for he would need all his strength to begin the next chapter of their journey.

In a few hours, Jack would return and by then Cobs would hopefully have hatched a plan. He needed to link a stolen soul, a dying man, and a hag with something to gain from it all. He knew one person in the house would have the answers he sought. But trying to wake him after such a party might not be the wisest of ideas and the thought of trying to talk to a giant Pumpkin head with a mischievous grin filled him with unrest.

Cobs took short hesitant steps up to the occupant's bedroom door and knocked very gently. The creature was a guest in his house so surely he would act accordingly. In truth, Cobs hoped his knock wouldn't be heard. That thought quickly evaporated when he heard the almighty crack of a whip. It struck the door and startled Cobs who stumbled backwards knocking over the fern on the hall table behind him. He waited a full minute before he plucked up the courage to knock again.

"Who in blazes is it at such an hour?"

Cobs had an overwhelming urge to run back to his room, hop back into his hammock and pull his patchwork quilt over his head. But no, important matters had to be discussed. The person he needed to talk to had ruled ruthlessly over the most unearthly creatures for centuries and witnessed things that would send fear into the hearts of many a Clurichaun. Cobs replied gingerly.

"Me."

"And who in blue blazes might 'me' be?"
"Me sir... I mean...Cobs sir."

The door flew open and two arms reached down and swept the tiny pointy-eared fellow straight of his feet. Cobs stared right in to the abyss that was the Dullahan's head then quickly glanced around the room. The pumpkin, that he had expected to see on the Dullahan's shoulders, lay cracked in two pieces on the floor. The Dullahan bellowed, "Can't even keep my head on straight."

Cobs laughed and soon the ground came up to meet him as the Dullahan set him back down.

"And what prey tell can be so urgent you needed to wake me from such a deep slumber?"

"I am truly sorry but Jack Turner is in grave danger."

Once Cobs began to explain everything that had happened he found it impossible to stop. "His father Matthew has been found and is back in Jack's cottage but he is at death's door. He woke for a brief moment and told Jack that his soul is trapped..." Cobs hesitated a moment, drew a deep breath and continued. "I thought that since you know all the evil..." he stopped, knowing that if he continued he would further offend the Dullahan and that is something he did not wish to do.

"I do not take insult at what you say little one." The Dullahan sat on the edge of his seat and seemed to look down at his boots. "In fact I am pleased you came to me. You say a soul has been stolen and a life hangs in the balance. I did not think that a mortal could exist without a soul."

"They cannot, but this is no ordinary mortal. Matthew Turner and Jack Turner are not exactly mortal." Cobs stood back knowing what reaction this would evoke when the penny dropped.

The Dullahan sprang to his feet and the heels of his boots dug deep into the floorboards. He clenched his fists and the seams of his leather gloves burst open. If the Dullahan had teeth, Cobs knew they would be broken now for the grinding sounds coming from the hollow space above the Dullahan's neck filled the bedroom with sounds worse than fingernails on a blackboard.

"I told Jack that he was born on a day of equal night and day and that he came from a long line of stone masons. I also told him he still had a special secret inside him that was more powerful than all the dandelions put together. I could sense it but not this...Jack Turner is a descendent of the longest oldest of stone masons... the Elderfolk? The very people who cast me and all like me into the Silver Orb, only to be forgotten for thousands of years. The years of turmoil and pain his kind put me through."

Cobs listened without interruption. He had learned that when someone was enraged like this it was better to let them vent. His mother Blaithnaid had taught him well. Whenever he had a tantrum as a child, she would never correct him until he had finished and calmed down again. 'There's no use talking to the horse as he's bolting and even less use after he's gone,' she used to say. It had taken Cobs at least two hundred years to understand what she meant. When the Dullahan had stopped shouting and Cobs could see the clenched fists unfurl he decided it was safe to talk.

"You forget that only for Jack and his selfless act you would still be in the Inner Realm. He wished for the Orb to break. You witnessed it. You cannot blame the boy for who his ancestors are no more than you can blame him for having curly hair or freckles."

The Dullahan let out an exasperated sigh. Cobs knew he had him on the run.

"You should remember the only reason Jack Turner set out on his quest was to get his father back safely but

98

when he witnessed the shared grief of all the creatures under that dome he sacrificed his hopes, dreams and wishes to set you all free. He saw that after the thousands of years of turmoil you described, you came to realise the only way to survive was to get along, to have mutual respect and understanding. I for one could not believe what I witnessed when I arrived that day at your Assembly in the Inner Realm. All those different creatures arguing with each other, but 'peacefully arguing' if there is such a thing. I saw no weapons, no fists, no fights."

The Dullahan slumped back down onto his chair. He had been defeated. He could not argue with Cobs. Jack Turner was a hero to all in the Inner Realm and the InBetween and that could never be undone.

"I apologise Cobs and please never tell Jack of this outburst. I am ashamed of myself," said the Dullahan.

"No need. It is only natural, but you are the better man to allow forgiveness." Cobs walked up to the Dullahan, he stood about the height of his knee and stared up into the eyes he imagined to be there.

"Will you help us?"

Chapter 15

Nightmare

Jack opened his eyes glad to be back in the familiar safety of his own room but immediately he was terror-struck. He grabbed for his eyes. They were open but he couldn't make anything out. He looked up to the rafters but he couldn't see them. He could see absolutely nothing.

He was blind.

Bile rose from his stomach and burned his throat as it exited his mouth. This could not be happening thought Jack. He couldn't be blind…he couldn't. Panic-struck he sat up and tried to focus on the other familiar surroundings of his bedroom, the cupboard, the door but something still blocked them from view. To his utter relief he realised his vision had not been impaired but this relief was short-lived, something else was in the room with him. This something else obstructed his sight. He reached out into the darkness and a million tiny insects landed on his bare arms. Jack wretched as the horrible sensation continued to travel towards his face. The swirling mass swarmed all over his bed.

He opened his mouth to scream…But nothing came out. His vocal chords were paralysed. No matter how hard he tried, nothing happened. He sat up further in the bed and despite his arms being covered with heaving creeping-crawling bugs he grabbed his own throat willing his vocal chords to work. All the while, the darkness began to get thicker and thicker until something started to reach out of the insect swarm. The seething mass began to merge into something that Jack could not believe. It merged into a long bony hand. He recognised the bony monstrosity, the thin veins, and the horrid yellow nails. It was something he knew he would never forget from the moment he shook hands with it...

Jack scrambled to find the fine silver necklace around his neck just as a thin frozen finger touched his skin. Thankfully, the necklace was still there. Frantically he fumbled round the back to where the Talisman hung. He grasped it tightly and let out a terrifying scream; a scream that would have frightened a Banshee.

"Maaaaaaa."

The creature's finger instantly turned back into darkness, a darkness made up of insects. Jack's scream combined with the power of the Talisman he held in his grip seemed to hurt the Hag. The window burst open and the insects escaped into the night. Then there was nothing.

Within seconds, Martha was standing by Jack's bedside beseeching her son to calm down.

"She was here Ma, she was here." A sweat covered Jack but he was cold to his mother's touch. His breathing was rapid and he was speaking so fast that Martha hardly understood a word he was saying.

"Calm down Jack. Calm down. You've had a nasty dream that's all." She drew Jack to her.

"She was here Ma I swear. And it wasn't a dream, it wasn't even a nightmare I tell you. It was as real as you are now."

"You're not making sense Jack. Who was here?" Martha clutched him to her breast. "It was a bad dream Jack, just a bad dream; they can't harm you now can they?"

Jack knew his mother must be right, there was no way it could be real. But when he lifted his head a fraction from her embrace and glanced over to the window two steely black globes of hatred stared back at him.

The Old Hag Doolen had been in his room.

She had tried to get him, tried to get the Talisman. The thought of her in possession of such a powerful object filled Jack with dread. He shivered from head to toe and his mother sensed this and held him even tighter. He snuggled into her warm chest but cast an eye back at the window. The horrifying eyes had gone.

Jack tried to take in everything that had just happened. A thought struck him: he knew his body would never be safe if he travelled back into Trom's. He would be fine in the InBetween but he couldn't guarantee he would live to tell the tale in his Outer Realm. He never thought it possible that he would be more at risk in his own world than that of one filled with creatures beyond his wildest imagination. What could he do? He had only come back to his body to stuff himself with as much food that he could last for a few days without having to wake. He had prepared for all the physical challenges his body would have to endure as he slept but it was worth it because on the other side of his bedroom wall lay the man who had raised him. That man stood taller than any giant in his eyes and his heart shone brighter than the Haulbowline

Lighthouse. There was nothing he wouldn't do for his father and some wicked old hag certainly wasn't going to stop him. All he needed was somewhere to hide whilst he slept and he knew the perfect place but it would be risky.

"Ma I'm sorry for being so silly. I don't know what I was thinking. You'd better go back to Da, he needs you more than me." Without hesitation, Jack ushered his mother out of the room convincing her that he just had a silly nightmare. He knew he had to act quickly if his plan was to succeed.

The instant his mother had gone, he sprang from his bed. Not knowing whether it was safer to hold onto the Talisman or hide it he opted to put it in the hidden compartment of the old wooden box under his bed. Once it was securely in place he darted to the living room and rifled through the food cupboard. Right at the very back, almost hidden from view was a large jar of prized honey. He knocked over several other jars in his haste to get it and he stuffed it into his backpack and tied a knot in the drawstring. He then ran to the front porch, grabbing his coat off the hook as he went and threw open the door. He was just in the nick of time for there in the distance was the outline of the flowing black mist. It was stealing away into the night and he knew he had to follow.

Jack sprinted down the hillside, running on the grass verge, staying away from the noisy gravel. He did not want to draw any attention to his stalking. He followed the black haze past the Old Mill. The Old Mill was the one place in the world next to his own house, where he felt safe but that was inside the building, in his special hiding place. He felt every bit as vulnerable standing outside at the corner wall peering round as the horrid sight just up ahead began to move again. He ran as quietly as he could along the shoreline making sure he kept a safe distance at all times. Suddenly the dark mist just up ahead came to an abrupt stop...

Jack had no choice and dived headlong into the darkness. To his relief he landed in a sand dune.

Had she heard him?

Did she know he was there all along?

Jack wished his heart would stop beating for if it was as loud outside of his head as it was inside then even his mother would have heard it back at the cottage. Then a thought struck him, why had the Doolen left just because his mother had entered the room? Surely the Hag could have stopped Martha if she wanted to. It gave him a lot to think about but now was not the time.

...The reason the evil shroud had stopped soon became evident. Jack could see it had reached the rusted high gates of the local graveyard. But now it looked as though the darkness was turning back towards him. Had the swarm sensed him? What could he do now? He held his breath even though his lungs begged him to inhale. But he knew in doing so he would give up his hiding place. The mist travelled back down the shoreline and stopped. It hovered inches away from his toes but after a brief moment, that seemed like more than a life time to Jack, the darkness moved on again, back towards the cemetery.

Now was his opportunity, his only chance. He sprang to his feet and raced along the thick bracken that lined the rest of the beach and all the while the shadowy blackness was just up ahead. It passed straight through the rusted bars of the old gate. Jack knew he couldn't dare open it for one creak and he would certainly be caught.

He could only watch hopelessly from his crouched position behind the bars. In a corner of the graveyard, he marvelled at the sight of the shadow as it began to get even darker if that were at all possible. Then it did the most horrific thing... it transformed into the Old Hag. Doolen had powers beyond anything Jack had ever imagined in his world. His was a world of boats and fields not shape shifting ancient insect hags. What on earth was going on?

Jack was familiar with the old graveyard. He skirted along the edge of the gate and just beyond it, behind some thick ivy, was a small gap in the old wall. He squeezed through and sprinted to a nearby rotten yew tree in a part of the graveyard he had never dared go into before. There were rumours of dogs and other animals wandering into that part of the cemetery and never returning home to their masters. They were never seen again, not even a skeleton, as if they vanished from the face of the earth. He pressed his back against the hollowed bark of the yew tree and waited.

Finally after what seemed an age and counting to ten for the umpteenth time he dared himself to peek around the other side of the tree to see what was going on. But after that particular count of ten he just sat there. He couldn't force himself to look. Fear gripped his heart too tightly.

The sound of rocks sliding over one another finally made Jack's mind up for him. Something was going on and he just had to know what it was. He poked his head out from his hiding place and instantly wished he hadn't. Doolen was now fully formed or as Jack thought fully 'deformed' and was standing next to the steps of a creepy abandoned family crypt. At least Jack thought it looked abandoned for it was decayed and crumbling. The kind of place grave robbers wouldn't even dare to go. The eerie stories about this part of the grave yard seemed all the more true now and death itself seemed to linger heavy here. He had never ventured this far before not even in the brightest of day light.

The uneven steps down into the crypt looked like they led all the way to Hell itself Jack thought. Goosebumps erupted all over his arms at his terrible thoughts and he bit his lower lip trying to control his imagination. It was running wild and he fought hard to bring it under control.

Jack stiffened as he watched Doolen disappearing from view as she descended the steps down into the crypt. The lid slid shut behind her. Only now did he feel safe enough to come out of hiding. She had gone from view and now was his only chance to move without her seeing him. He slowly edged his way up to the grave.

So this is where she hid. It was still dark so maybe she would wait a while and go back to his cottage to try and get the Talisman. Now he felt vulnerable for not having it on him. He couldn't fully understand why but he knew it had offered him some kind of protection. Hadn't it? Or was it calling out to his mother that frightened the Hag off? Doolen hadn't stayed to fight his mother but he was grateful she hadn't.

He hadn't any more time to think of what might have happened for the tomb suddenly opened again and a deathly night shadow lifted from within. It moved across the graveyard heading back up the hill. Jack was in no doubt where it was heading but he had other ideas at that precise moment.

With his heart in his throat, Jack darted from the shelter of the tree towards the tomb. The lid was closing over as he approached. He increased his pace and leapt into the air gliding past the lid of the tomb just as it slammed shut. Then complete darkness surrounded him. There was no way back now. He had to be brave and hope he had made the right decision. Down below on the floor of the tomb a flicker of dim light beckoned.

Jack took small tentative steps down the stone steps and he entered the shelter of the Old Hag. The floor was strewn with the bones of what must have been hundreds of cats and dogs. So the rumours were true thought Jack.

In the centre of the underground vault stood a huge black iron cauldron; thick grey curls of smoke spilled out over the rim. The room's walls were bare and smooth; black as marble and icy cold to the touch. On one wall Jack could see a small shelf. He stood on his tiptoes and peered over the lip of the shelf and resting there in a thick layer of dust were two small spiky balls. Each ball glowed blood-red from within. Jack recognised them immediately. They were two halves of a Talisman. It resembled his in every way except in colour. Something inside him told him that the pieces of the Talisman held a great danger. He could not fully understand what he felt but he knew he dared not touch them so he lowered himself back down to the floor.

To give himself some comfort he placed his open palm over his trouser pocket and sure enough it was there as it always was; his birthday present; his tiny boat. But now he had a new gift in his possession. Now he had his Obsidian stone. To anyone else it just looked like a worry-stone but rubbing the stone was not calming him down. Even with these precious objects in his possession it didn't have the desired effect. Jack was utterly alone and powerless.

There was nothing else in the room, no place to hide as he'd hoped. He knew the last place that the Old Hag would look for him was in her own hidey-hole. That is why he'd followed her there in the first place. Now it didn't seem like such a good idea. All he wanted now was to be out of there and safely tucked up in his bed. But his bed was the first place he knew Doolen would go. She would probably be there by now, surprised by his absence.

He looked around the room again hoping he'd missed something and there it was staring out at him all along. On the bottom step was an inscription and it read.

THE ORB WILL FALL AND MANKIND WITH IT

A sense of dread filled Jack. It was he who had made the Orb fall... what had he got to do with the fate of all humankind?

Now he had an urgent need to get out of there. Had he made a dreadful mistake? He felt he had leapt from a hot griddle plate into the fire and he began to panic. There had to be a way out. He ran up the stone steps to the lid of the tomb and began to bang furiously but it was no good.

All he achieved were two sore fists and an eyeful of dust. He slumped down on the top step and began to cry. Was this to be his final resting place? He knew his death would be imminent. If the Hag never returned, he would be left to starve to death and if she did return she would certainly kill him.

The minutes crept by so slowly until finally they became hours and they continued to drag on until Jack lost all sense of time. Just as he was about to reach into his back pack to get some of the honey he had taken from the cottage there was an unbearable scraping overhead. Jack threw his hands to his ears to block out the sound as he looked up. The stone lid of the tomb slid across and sharp rays of light stabbed the darkness. Without a moment's hesitation, Jack ran back down the steps taking them two at a time, he dived behind the giant cauldron and cowered down awaiting his fate.

A thick sweeping swarm of insects, silent as night and devoid of any light entered the chamber. The familiar stench carried by the Shimnavore filled the air. Without even knowing it Jack had put his hand in his pocket and was rubbing the Obsidian stone for all he was worth. He tried to control his tremors as he waited for Doolen's icy cold hands to be wrapped around his throat but to his utter surprise they never came.

She hadn't seen him.

As the cloud brushed over to the other side of the room, Jack inhaled deeply and took his chance.

It was now or never.

He sprang to his feet and bolted up the stone steps and back into the early morning sunlight. He made straight for the hollowed out yew tree and took shelter there until the lid of the tomb shut firmly. He had made it or so he thought. A blood curdling scream emanated from below the ground, a scream so loud that the lid of the tomb cracked. Jack knew the end had come. But nothing more happened. Nothing burst out from the grave. Then it dawned on him the reason she didn't appear was the early morning sunlight. It had to be her weakness.

With a renewed hope Jack headed for his favourite hiding place. He hoped the Old Hag would never think to look for him there.

Jack ran from the graveyard and made home. Without disturbing his mother he got the Talisman from the box under his bed then he went to the one place that he felt safe; his second home: the Old Mill. He edged his way round the side of the building and found the familiar small wooden flap that the flour bags would come out. He was in luck for the flap had not been secured so he was able to creep inside. He quickly made his way up the long ladder that extended the whole height of the mill, from the tiled floor to the dizzying heights above until he found his dark place in the attic. Once he was securely in place he lifted the ladder up with him so no one else could climb up and get him. He buried himself under a mound of straw and opened his backpack and lifted out the honey, opened the jar and quickly filled his mouth with fistfuls of the sweet syrup. When the jar was empty, he threw it to one side, shoved his damp sticky fingers into his pockets, and lifted out the two joined up sections of his precious Talisman. He placed it around his neck as the book had demonstrated and lay back on the floor boards hoping that sleep would come fast. Given that he had just run for his life and that he hadn't slept properly for days he quickly fell into a deep slumber.

Chapter 16

Pact

"Cobs, Cobs," Jack called out. He opened his eyes and stared up at an intricately carved oak ceiling depicting scenes from a summer day in the hills. "I'm back. Where are you?"

Jack had returned to Trom's body and he desperately needed to find Cobs and tell him all that had taken place since he had left.

He hopped down from the hammock as if he'd done it a million times before. There must be some memories in Trom's body that helped him because the last time he slept in a hammock he ended up falling out and landing very ungracefully onto a mattress. He ran to the door and was about to shout out for Cobs again but he realised, almost too late, that he might call too much attention to himself. He knew his eyes would give him away so he walked along the corridors on tip toes. The house was still ghostly quiet except for a room up ahead on the left where he was sure he could hear something. He pressed his ear up against the door and grinned. He recognised Cobs voice.

"Cobs," he whispered and rapped on the door gently.

"Who is there?" shouted the Dullahan.

"It's me," replied Jack.

"Me who?" asked Cobs.

"Cobs. For goodness sake open the bloomin' door and let me in."

Cobs ran to the door and opened it. Jack toppled into the room, stumbled across the floor and when he looked up he was staring at the underside of the Dullahan's boot.

"What is the meaning of this intrusion?" the Dullahan   demanded.

"Not again," said Jack. "The last time I saw the underside of your boot you were about to stomp on my head. It was then that the Dullahan saw the familiar eyes looking out from Trom's sockets.

"Jack my boy. It is you. Cobs has been telling me all about your exploits but nothing about this. How is this possible young man? You are in another's body and you are controlling it."

Suddenly the Dullahan shifted uncomfortably in his seat. If he had a head, it would have had a furrowed brow and a deeply concerned look upon its face but since it did not have either a brow or a face Cobs and Jack could tell from the way he moved: body language some people call it.

"You are wearing both pieces of the Talisman of Salix aren't you?"

"Yes of course I am. Cobs told me to. Why what's wrong with that? How else would I be able to get around?"

The Dullahan moved closer to Jack and asked him to take a seat. Jack obliged him sensing, from his tone, that something was gravely wrong.

"Jack, I have much to tell you. And you as well Cobs. Join us," said the Dullahan.

Cobs hopped up beside Jack. He looked very nervous. He was the one who had told Jack to wear both pieces of the Talisman in the first place.

The Dullahan let out a huge sigh and began...

"I have shared the hills with Banshees," said the Dullahan, "eaten foraged feasts with Merrows and, even against my better judgement, sought the advice of ancient Changelings but never have I thought I would have to do this."

The Dullahan put his hands up over his faceless face and sighed again. Cobs could see that whatever the Dullahan was thinking it could not be any more serious.

Cobs had sensed the InBetween was in severe danger and now he knew the Dullahan was aware of it too. The Dullahan continued...

"My kind and all the other creatures like me had free reign over Ireland but we grew cocky and treated mankind like they were beneath us. They live for such a brief period, nothing more than a heartbeat in the eyes of many. We tormented them; ruined their crops, spoiled their milk, caused mayhem whenever the chance arose and all for our own pleasure. This went on for centuries, if not millennia.

I remember the day the sky suddenly darkened and I thought it was just grey clouds gathering but they were not clouds, they were the giant arks of stone; gigantic granite ships floating on an ocean of air. They heralded our demise. The ships were captained by a race called The Elderfolk. A race of man-like creatures, ancient beings of skin and bone with huge heads as pale as ash and draped in a fine luminous mesh that resembled chain mail. Each one of them had two enormous obsidian black eyes with twinkling veins of white running horizontally through them like quartz.

Their King called himself Blianta. "

Jack's eyes widened at the mention of the name. He had heard it before somewhere. He wracked his mind until finally he remembered. The old Hag Doolen had mentioned that name in the graveyard at his Nanna Tess' funeral. Jack didn't say a word, he knew better than to interrupt the Dullahan.

The Dullahan continued. "Blianta summoned all our kinds together to plead with us stop us wreaking havoc on the humans. He called it 'The Calling.'

I was the only one who attended. I think I was the only one who recognised the importance of his words. I was the only one to meet Blianta at 'The Calling'. He was angry at being ignored by all the others, I could tell as soon as I met him. But soon he calmed and we spoke at great length. He told me how his people had seen what was to become of Ireland. They had the gift of foresight and they could not let what they saw come to pass. He told me the Elderfolk held immense power and they were about to use it to bring about order. I tried to convince them that we could change but I alone was not enough. Blianta was enraged at our arrogance, he saw only one option, and he took it.

He ordered the building to commence.

Blianta told me how his kind had travelled for eons through storms of time and oceans of emptiness to get to our shores but in doing so, some of his people were driven mad. The endless travel through The Rivers of Naught affected their minds. It twisted their pure thoughts until all they craved was chaos. His tribe split into two factions. They fought amongst themselves until the inevitable happened.

There was mutiny... and a new race calling themselves 'The Ancients' or 'The Old Ones' as they were also known began to helm the other ships of rock. They looked the same as the Elderfolk except for one small detail; their eyes were pure Obsidian, full of darkness. There was no dazzling white line in them. The Ancients took great delight in what they found when they arrived in Ireland and the more mayhem they witnessed the stronger they seemed. They became crazed and the Elderfolk could see this.

So the Elderfolk began to build faster...

...They built...

The Mourne Wall.

It took the Elderfolk two years to build it and would have taken man nearly twenty. It enclosed the highest peaks, through Tors of bare rock and into the lowest valleys, crossing fifteen mountains; over the rugged slopes of Binnian, Commedagh and Donard to name but a few."

The Dullahan barely paused for breath as he continued to unburden his dark secret.

"No one could comprehend the absolute power the wall held. It looked like any other dry stone wall but Blianta, the mighty king of the Elderfolk, explained what it was for. It was to be a prison for all my kind. I could not dissuade him and that is when I had only one option. I pleaded with him. I made a pact. Blianta bestowed me with a limited power over all the evil creatures that would reside within the wall and that power would last for thousands of years. In return, he would lock the Ancients, The Old Ones, away from us, inside the mountain beyond an impassable road under a spell and there they would remain until the Silver Orb was broken.

The Elderfolk used their power to banish all my kind inside the wall and seal us within the Silver Orb. Then they created a second Orb to separate the Outer Realm from where we sit now. They made the three realms: the Outer Realm, the InBetween and the Inner Realm.

Blianta's fatal mistake was changing his mind. He thought that such a show of power would bring the Ancients to their senses and they would not need to be cast into the Inner Realm.

The Elderfolk had given the Ancients a chance to change, an opportunity to live in the InBetween with the other races. But the making of the Orbs had the opposite effect. Instead, the Ancients saw it as a great sign of weakness and they created the single most evil creature to walk this earth...

... The Shimnavore. "

Cobs inhaled deeply when he saw for the first time in the Dullahan's story he recognised the Shimnavore as the reviled creature he fought so valiantly not days before.

"So what happened?" asked Jack.

"The Shimnavore grew more ruthless and slaughtered everything in sight. The Elderfolk tried to fight them but the Ancients had thought of everything. The Shimnavore were born of the River Shimna and they were impenetrable to any of the Elderfolk's weapons or spells or powers. However, the Shimnavore had designs of their very own. They were deadly and they killed as many of the Ancients, who created them, as they did Elderfolk. That is when a decision was made by the Elderfolk Council to open the unbreachable Mourne Wall, to cast the Shimnavore inside."

Jack interrupted. "I was told that the Shimnavore killed all the Ancients and that is why they were cast inside the wall. But how can you break an impenetrable wall?"

"You cannot," replied the Dullahan. "That is what gave rise to the Holocene. The Elderfolk unleashed the greatest power they had ever harnessed and they were successful in ending the war. The Ancients and Shimnavore were trapped inside the wall but the release of such energy wiped the Elderfolk out. They had hoped it would only breach the Mourne Wall for an instant but instead the very mountains were torn apart. The Wall and the Silver Orb became warped and the Orb never healed. It had a weakness. It had a hole in it. The Shimnavore exploited this fact when they found out. They could come into the InBetween but they were wise to remain hidden from the remainder of the Elderfolk."

Jack interrupted again. "But you said it destroyed all the Elderfolk. They were all wiped out."

"There was only a handful left, of which Blianta was one."

"But you were inside the Orb how could you know this." Cobs looked puzzled.

"That too was part of the pact. Blianta and I became linked. He used the Talisman to bind our two spirits. He said each half of Talisman could link two people's spirits. But if the two halves were worn by the one person then madness would soon follow and they would be lost in someone else's mind. The power was far too great for one mind alone. Normally half a Talisman could only be worn by a member of the Elderfolk but Blianta knew of a way for me to wear it. It had something to do with my head not being attached to my body."

Cobs looked worried at hearing this. He knew Jack had been wearing both pieces of the Talisman just as he had instructed him to do but he never for a moment realised the danger. Lost in someone else's mind, a mind that was fighting back, fighting for dominance, just like when he was insulted by Trom after Jack sang in the Dining Hall. How long would it take before the wearer would be damaged permanently? Cobs jumped down from his seat and stared up at Jack.

"I am so, so, sorry Jack. I had no idea of the danger I put you in. I had noticed you acting a bit strangely but I promise I never thought anything I advised could have harmed you. You must believe me."

Cobs' face was wracked with guilt and Jack could see this.

"Of course I know Cobs. We've been through so much and you've saved my life countless times," said Jack.

"You must take the Talisman off Jack. You have no choice."

"No I will not. Not until I have done what I have come here to do."

To Cobs' amazement, he saw no concern on Jack's face. Trom's features remained calm. For a moment, Cobs thought that maybe expression was one feature that couldn't be shared, but Jack soon proved him wrong. He raised one eyebrow and the other dropped. Once again Cobs could see sarcasm painted on his friend's face even if he was looking at Trom's.

"Do you hear me Jack? No one was ever to wear both pieces of the Talisman," said the Dullahan. "They were to be shared so two spirits would be linked. It was never designed for one creature to take over another's. If you do this for a prolonged period not only will your own body perish but the body you take over will be driven mad. This cannot go on."

"All I want is to get my father's soul returned to him so he can be whole again and come back to me and my mother," said Jack. "I know he can't hang on for much longer. It's been a few days now and he can't last. I need to know what I can do."

Jack got up and started rubbing his hands together. Cobs quickly noticed it. He'd never ever seen Jack do that before and it worried him. This was something that Trom did when he was excited Had the change already begun? Could Jack be in mortal danger back in his own realm? But now did not seem like the time to discuss his concerns.

The Dullahan continued, "Blianta wore one half and I the other. He said all the Elderfolk wore half a Talisman and it connected one to another. They were 'Kindred Spirits'. Each stone held different properties. He said that the Ancients, even though they were driven mad, still kept the link to the Elderfolk. Even through the Orb we could hear each other's thoughts but for some reason the link did not last. We spoke to one another for thousands of years and then about a hundred years ago nothing. Something happened. The last word I ever heard Blianta speak screamed across my mind. I don't know what it meant but I never heard from him again."

"What was the word?" asked Jack trying hard not to fidget with his hands.

"What could it matter little one?"

"Please. It does matter. What was the word?"

"Doolen," the Dullahan answered.

Jack gasped.

Chapter 17

Now it begins

"I have an idea Cobs but we need to go back to your father's study to look at something first," said Jack.

The three friends rose up and headed straight to the hidden room. The fire as always blazed in the hearth and the pictures of Cobs the Bear stared down from sketches and paintings on the walls. The family portrait behind the giant overstuffed sofa seemed to show faces that looked happier than before, if that were at all possible. But then again in this realm, many things were possible; rocks rose out of rivers to save young lives, castles appeared out of thin air just by crossing your eyes, heathers held secrets and this only scraped the surface of this world. It was truly a remarkable place, a distant place, a place apart.

Jack approached the bureau in the corner of the study and pressed on its sides. Nothing happened.

"Not like that Jack, "said Cobs. He sidled up to him, bent down, and hit a panel in the corner with his fist. It sprang open. Inside sat a small black pot. Jack remembered it from when he first met Cobs. That seemed so long ago now. It amazed him how such a short space of time he could make a friend-for-life.

Jack ignored the pot and lifted out the old leather manuscript; The Book of the Elderfolk.

"I don't think my father would take too kindly to us knowing that this is here Jack," said Cobs.

"Well then, keep an eye on the door and make sure no one comes in."

"I'll do better than that," said the Dullahan and he jammed his whip into the latch of the door so no one could enter. "Now we have as much time as we like."

Jack drummed his index fingers on the cover of the book in just the same way Trom did and Cobs realised they might not have as much time as they all thought. Jack was in real danger.

Jack placed the Book of the Elderfolk on the bureau and opened to the first page. The writing was truly wonderful. The first letter engraved into the parchment depicted a winged creature none of them had ever seen before. It appeared to be from another world or at the very least another time. It did not belong to the InBetween, the Outer Realm, or even the now shattered Inner Realm. The words on the page were unfathomable, not written in a language any of them could decipher.

"There's only one thing I want to know," said Jack staring at the pages.

Then something very strange happened right in front of Jack's eyes. The symbols on the page seemed to dance about, letter slipped over letter, weaving in and out like the ocean's tides. He rubbed his eyes thinking the lack of sleep his own body had could be affecting Trom but that wasn't it. The words shifted, swam once more, and finally fell into a new order. Then the voices began. They started to speak all at once. Jack put his hands to his ears. It was all too much to bear.

"Are you alright Jack," asked Cobs concerned at seeing his friend in such a terrible state.

"Can't you hear them Cobs? They're all speaking at once. I cannot take it."

Cobs shut the book quickly and the voices in Jack's head stopped instantly.

"Are you alright Jack?"

"Yes, I can hear myself think now. But we have no choice. Nanna Tess copied the words from this book into her letters; the ones I found and they helped bring me here. She said the book spoke to her too and now I understand what she meant."

Jack rubbed his face with his open hands and breathed deeply. He stared at the cover of the book: three fish embossed were on the cover and as he looked at them they began to shift, to move over one another and Jack just knew that he was the only one who could see it.

The book somehow knew him. Then it dawned on him. Of course it knew him. It was written for his kind.

The Book of the Elderfolk.

No wonder he could hear it speak. The book was crying out to the last of the Elderfolk. Jack placed his hand on the cover and although it seemed silly, he leaned in close and whispered to it.

"I can only hear you if you speak one at a time. There are many pages to look at and I know one holds the answer but help me, please."

Cobs and the Dullahan knew they were witnessing something truly remarkable and they kept their silence.

Cautiously Jack opened the great book but this time rather than being bombarded by a thousand voices all shouting louder than the other in a fight to be heard, a hush of silenced whispers reached his ears. They were talking in unison and all saying the same thing. The words flowed across Jack's mind. The writing was so familiar. It looked just like his Nanna Tess'.

Now you have found us abandon us not

We the ignored for so long

Ask of us anything and we shall reward you

With the answers you seek

Jack placed his hands flat on the bureau's surface, one on either side of the book. He closed his eyes and in his mind he asked his question.

'Where is my father's soul?'

Then he opened them. To his astonishment, the book began to quiver and then shake a little more and a little more until all at once the pages began to flick over as fast as he'd ever seen. It was though an invisible hand was searching for the answer to Jack's question. The pages became a blur and as they turned words leapt up until finally they slowed down and came to an abrupt stop. A single page lay opened, halfway through the huge tome. Jack flicked over the pages on either side of the one the book stopped at but they were all blank. They had been erased. Jack wanted to know how this happened as did Cobs and the Dullahan who watched over his shoulder in bewilderment. However, the only page of any importance was the one the book had stopped at, everything else seemed irrelevant.

A detailed sketch of a mountain path lay on the centre of the page. The words written beneath the picture only Jack could understand. He looked over his shoulder to the Dullahan and Cobs.

"Do either of you know where this is?"

The Dullahan turned his back on Jack but Cobs replied, "I've never seen it before. Do you even know what it says Jack?"

"Oh yes. It is telling me that beyond this place is the All-Seer. I don't know who or what that is but from their name they sound like they might have answers. It says beyond here is where the souls of every Elderfolk who fell in battle during and since the Holocene are held captive waiting for the next great storm."

Jack slammed the book shut. "Something isn't right Cobs; in fact something is very wrong."

Cobs placed a hand on his friend's shoulder and held it there, saying nothing. The Dullahan became obvious with his silence. Jack looked at Cobs and whispered quietly too him. He knew how softly he could speak and Cobs' huge pointed ears would pick up what he said.

"What's wrong with the Dullahan?" asked Jack.

"I think he knows something but is too afraid to say," answered Cobs.

"The Dullahan afraid? Something must be wrong for him to be ill at ease. Ask him," said Cobs.

"No, you," taunted Jack.

"No, you. I said it first."

The Dullahan turned, his long dark leather cloak swished as he moved. "Stop your petty bickering you two. I can hear as well as any pointy-eared Leprechaun."

"Clurichaun," snapped Cobs, his fists pressed into his hips.

Jack shouted, "So help me Dullahan I'll find that head of yours and when I do I'll take great pleasure in kicking it round like a child's ball."

"Now who's bickering," said Jack trying to calm the tension in the room.

"Just keeping you on your toes," said the Dullahan. "I'm afraid I know where the place in the book is. It's just I never thought..." He stopped mid sentence as if he couldn't go on.

"Where is it?" said Jack through gritted teeth. "You have to tell me. My father's life depends on it.

The Dullahan replied sternly. "That is the impassable road. The road that no one can ever travel...

...The Devil's Coachroad.

Chapter 18

Tonight

In her tomb, deep underground, the Old Hag Doolen paced the floor. Jack Turner would not see the morning if she had her way. Once the strong sun began to fade, she would leave her hiding place and come find him even if that meant breaking into his house. It no longer mattered who saw her for she didn't care who knew of her existence. For too long she hid in the shadows, searching, forever searching until her time came and she waited for the perfect moment. Tess' death was that moment. Now not Martha or any mortal would stop her from taking what she desired and using Jack in her despicable plan.

A few thousand years ago Doolen would have been happy just to go back to her realm. Go back and take her rightful place. She had thought for more than two hundred generations that she was the only one of her kind in the Outer Realm for never in all that time had she met anyone else like her.

Then everything changed when she found Blianta, the King of the Elderfolk. After years of wandering the planet she found him in Ireland in a small village called Bryansford, right next to Tollymore Forest.

It was Blianta who had unleashed the power stored in the great Cloc Mor Stone and in doing so he was closest to the mammoth explosion of the Holocene. The shockwave was so powerful it threw him into the Outer

Realm. Doolen had been close to the explosion too for she had run from the marauding Shimnavore, a creature she helped to create. She had gone to beg for refuge with the King. But before she could plead for her life the explosion caught her and cast her out. Banished her to a world where she lived in exile.

Killing Blianta was so easy for her. He did not sense her approach. How he died is too scary for a book of this nature but it is enough to say it was horrible and that will save you from a lifetime of nightmares.

But Doolen quickly realised her terrible mistake. When she held up her Talisman it was no longer glowing white but had turned blood-red. It was now tainted by Blianta dying at her hands. Then she saw the damaged Talisman around Blianta's neck. His death destroyed his Talisman as well.

The last word he spoke was her name.

The day Tess returned from the InBetween everything changed for Doolen. Now the old hag had a glimmer of hope. The Talisman Tess had brought with her called out to Doolen. It was then that Doolen realised Tess was a member of the Elderfolk for only they could hold such a precious item. It would bring instant death to any mere mortal. Doolen knew then that not only had some of the Elderfolk lived on after the Holocene in the Outer Realm; they had taken human form, just as she had done, and lived among the humans even to the point where they had families of their own.

Now Doolen wanted everything, a place on the highest throne ruling over all three of the worlds. She knew the Silver Orb had been shattered, she felt that in her very core. Jack Turner had done that much for her. Now all she needed was a Talisman to give her back her strength. She wanted a full Talisman to unleash the power inside her. This is what the Ancient's had done on the crossing to Ireland all those millennia ago. They got bored and restless and decided to do what their Kings forbade. They placed two halves of their Talismans together and wore them as one. The new power they held was so thrilling, all consuming. They could control other beings, create creatures from nothing, and breathe life into them. In their hunger for more and more power they did not notice their fall into madness. It takes the eyes of others to recognise that.

Now Doolen wanted a new body, a strong young body and she would have the pick of the best once she had Jack Turner's Talisman. Now all she needed to do was get her hands on the boy.

Unbeknownst to anyone Jack Turner lay in a deep sleep in a tiny attic corner of the Corn Mill. But all the while the Talisman he wore called out. It called out to anyone who knew what to listen for. And someone could hear that call, sense its aura beckoning. Now it would only be a matter of hours before the sun went down and the Old Hag would be free to track down the voices she heard. She would finally get her hands on the Talisman but more importantly she would have Jack Turner in her grasp.

Jack was essential to her plan.

At least his soul was...

Chapter 19

Coachroad

A frenzied panic struck Jack as he stood in the study. There was much to do. He had found the path that would lead to his father's rescue. His father's soul lay beyond that 'Coachroad' and no matter what they called it, 'Devil' or otherwise it didn't scare him. He couldn't wait to set off into the mountains to find it. Jack grabbed Cobs by the wrist and tugged him.

"Let's go."

"What?" replied Cobs. He resisted Jack tugging on his arm for all he was worth but Trom's body was stronger than he imagined.

"Stop it Jack," he shouted. "You're hurting me."

Jack let him go and looked down to Cobs' forearm. He could see the red finger marks on his pale skin and he flinched for a second.

"Wait... Wait... for what? A written invitation?"

Cobs looked very worried. Even with Jack's frustration he would never have been this physical before and for that matter neither would Trom... but combined. He forced the thought from his mind.

"Then stay here Cobs I don't need you."

Cobs slumped to the floor in stunned silence. This wasn't the Jack he knew. The frustrations were showing themselves in a whole new way and he didn't like it.

Jack looked at the Dullahan. "You say you know where this place is so there isn't a minute to lose."

"It isn't as simple as that Jack. There are a few things you need to know first," said the Dullahan calmly.

"I agree," added Cobs finding his voice. "You must listen before you go off half-cocked."

Jack stamped his foot. "I don't care what you say. I just want my father back. Now come on Dullahan."

Jack turned and headed out the door expecting to hear heavy footsteps behind him but none came. He spun round and threw his hands in the air when he saw that neither companion had moved.

"You are going about this the wrong way Jack," said the Dullahan.

This comment only fuelled Jack's rage further. He squeezed his fists together until his fingernails dug deeply into his palms. Then he let loose. He charged at the Dullahan, his arms flying and he threw punch after punched on the massive thigh above the Dullahan's knee. It caused no pain to the Dullahan and he let Jack continue to beat him.

After a minute of rage-driven torment Jack fell to the ground, exhausted. Even in Trom's body he hadn't managed to get a reaction from the Dullahan for he had known the boy needed to work out his frustrations. Then Cobs heard the sobs.

Cobs knelt down beside Jack.

"We will do everything to help you but you can't run in with a sword at the ready to a fight that needs much more. You'll be annihilated. Jack there is one thing we haven't told you. I only found out myself this morning."

Jack wiped the back of his sleeve under his nose and he tried hard to stop crying for long enough to hear to what Cobs had to say. He felt defeated enough without yet another obstacle in his way.

"There's something about the Devil's Coachroad Jack," interrupted the Dullahan and it is only right I tell you."

Jack stopped sniffling and listened attentively.

"Jack, you told me back in the Inner Realm, when we were all still trapped, that you knew there was a hole in the Silver Orb and that was how the Shimnavore were able to cross the Mourne Wall and get their claws on the dandelion clocks. Do you remember?"

"Of course I do," said Jack.

"Do you remember what I told you then?"

"Mmmmm," said Jack.

"I told you that the Elderfolk put a curse on the Wall and even if the Shimnavore or any other captive did get out they couldn't live for long."

"Yes I remember you saying that. You said that explained why the Shimnavore must have disappeared."

"Well I wasn't being entirely honest with you Jack."

Jack jumped to his feet. Honesty was one thing but this was more of a revelation. Cobs sat up too. This was news to him too and he couldn't wait to hear what was coming next.

"The Elderfolk's curse forced any creature who ever breached the Wall to walk the Devil's Coachroad."

Jack began to stand up. He wiped the tears from his eyes and tried to make sense of all he had heard. He couldn't blame the captives of the Silver Orb for hating his people. His people. It was the first time he thought of himself like that. He was a member of the Elderfolk. He was not human, well not fully.

"So what is it you have to tell me?" said Jack.

"You cannot walk the Devil's Coachroad," said the Dullahan. It was as if a weight had been removed from his shoulders. He had revealed a secret he held inside for thousands of years but this didn't help Jack.

"Why not?" shouted Jack. "Who's going to stop me?"

"It's not like that. That is why we have to plan. No one can walk the Devil's Coachroad. The path is not just treacherous. There is more to the curse placed on it."

"I don't care," shouted Jack.

"Will you shut up and listen boy," the Dullahan roared back for he had run out of patience. "You cannot walk the Devil's Coachroad...No one can walk the Coachroad."

"No one?" said Jack almost in stunned silence.

"No one that is... no one with a soul," answered the Dullahan.

It took a few moments for what he heard to sink in. A body with a soul could not walk the Coach Road. His mind raced. How could he reach the souls on the other side? How did they get there? But most of all, how could he free his father?

He sat down again quickly and placed a hand on either side of the great book then asked his second question.

"How can someone walk the Devil's Coachroad?"

The leaves of the book began to quiver once more. The book began to shake and suddenly the pages fluttered all the way from one side of the book to the other, growing ever faster. From cover to cover, back to back. They became a blur but after a while they still did not stop and Jack knew...

He put his hand out and stopped the pages from going through another cycle.

They did not hold the answer. So this time Jack had to ask himself. 'How can I walk the Devil's Coachroad if I have a soul? The answer is simple. I cannot. I cannot walk the Devil's Coachroad if I have a soul. He repeated this over and over in his mind. Time and time again he said it. I cannot, I cannot, I cannot. If I have a soul... if I have a soul...if I have a soul...'

'What if...'

Then it suddenly clicked. Things fell into place inside his head and Jack grinned.

Chapter 20

Swarm

The summer sun began to fade and a dark mist shrouded the jagged back of Carrick Little Mountain. A storm was coming.

A violent CRACK exploded through the graveyard and shook the ground as the lid on Doolen's tomb fractured and split in two. Each half catapulted into the air and from within the bowels of the earth a plague of insects was unleashed. The winged infestation coiled up into the air then blazed forward over the land ravaging everything in its wake. Summer grass was scorched and blackened, gravestones disintegrated, trees burned and fell. A rancid power unseen on earth devoured nature's beauty. The swarm surged on until it reached the door of Jack Turner's cottage where it stopped, hovering at the entrance. The smell of burned seaweed filled the air choking the flowers growing around the archway. They drooped and fell.

From the insect-mist of blackness stepped the Old Hag Doolen. She crossed to Jack's bedroom window and peered in but she couldn't see him there. He must be hiding she thought. She could sense the Talisman and knew it was close. She could feel it. Her anger grew with every second that passed; the Talisman was within her grasp. She went back to the front door and knocked heavily but there was no answer. She could stand it no longer and manners were certainly not going to stand in her way. She lifted her boot and kicked the front door with a fraction of her strength. It burst off its hinges and hurtled end over end through the living room and crashed against the door of Jack's parent's room. Martha was inside nursing Matthew; she jumped to her feet at the sound of the terrible commotion outside her door. As scared as she was and without asking who was there, she opened her door but she did not expect to find what she did.

Standing in the middle of the living room with a long scowling face was the Old Hag Doolen. A dark mist licked round her feet and once Martha realised what it was made up of she did everything in her power not to look down again.

Martha trembled visibly but still she managed to ask, "What are you doing here? I told you the last time we met that I would let you know if we came across that trinket you sought."

"Don't try to fool me woman. Now where is that urchin child of yours?"

Martha resisted the urge to defend her son from the hag's name calling however there was no way she would ever reveal his whereabouts. But her eyes gave her away as she glanced over to his room.

"Ahhh, hiding in his room as I thought." She approached Martha and her bony hand grabbed for her neck. Martha stepped to one side and ran to Jack's door and threw herself against it.

"There's no way I'm letting you in here. Not over my dead body you old Hag. Now get out of my house."

"No need to get personal my dear. All I want is something that belongs to me..." Doolen cackled. "Oh, and something that belongs to you."

Within a blink of Martha's eye Doolen had crossed the room and was looking up into her eyes. The frail Old Hag would not get the better of her and she stood her ground.

"Did you not hear me? I'm not afraid of you if that's what you think. Now get out of my house."

Doolen cackled even louder this time and she reached up, a filthy bony hand extended from the shredded sleeve of her cape and her fingers enveloped Martha's throat. Martha could not believe the superhuman strength of the Hag but the icy cold pain that accompanied it rendered her defenceless. Martha coughed and spluttered as her throat was being slowly crushed. She fought harder and harder for each breath and just as she thought she would breathe no more the Hag tossed her against the wall like a cross child with a toy that was no longer of interest. Martha knew nothing more after that for the impact knocked her unconscious.

Doolen ransacked the cottage, leaving nothing undisturbed but she found neither the boy nor the Talisman. But she sensed something was in the cottage. Objects from the InBetween were different from the Outer Realm but only someone like her noticed. What she thought was the Talisman that belonged to the Elderfolk were actually Tess' writings in the cupboard. They held a power that the Doolen had not felt for a long time so it was no wonder she had mistaken them for that of the Talisman. She stuffed the pages into the folds of her cloak and she continued on. She even searched Matthew as he lay on his deathbed. Were there no lengths to which this unscrupulous demon would not sink?

Finally satisfied what she sought was not in the cottage she left, but not before getting her final revenge. She clicked her finger and thumb together and a spark ignited. She then pointed her index finger up into the rafters and flame burst forth immediately setting fire to the dry thatch. Within seconds, it blazed furiously over the heads of Martha and Matthew. They lay oblivious to their peril and the mad cackling coming deep from within the murky insect-fog swept out the front door. The Doolen had picked up the aura of the InBetween again and this time she would not be fooled. She was closing in on Jack Turner. She could feel it. It would not be long before the Hag had his throat in her grasp.

Chapter 21

Husk

Jack watched Cobs prepare for another outing into the Mourne Mountains. He sat on the floor, crossed his legs and placed his hands on his knees, drumming his fingers.

"Stop that Trom..." barked Cobs. " You know how much that annoys me." He looked into Jack's eyes in horror. "Sorry Jack I never meant to shout like that."

"No problem Cobs. I'm sorry. I wasn't even aware I was doing it. I think I must have been daydreaming for a moment."

"No Jack, I shouldn't have shouted like that, it's just... Oh never mind."

Now was not a good time for Cobs to point out what Jack was doing. They were headed out on a new quest only this time however it was different for both of them as neither knew the paths they would be walking; they were venturing into what was previously the Inner Realm, a place not yet explored by Clurichauns or anyone else from the InBetween. All they knew was their destination; The Devil's Coachroad. But before they would arrive there they had to visit an old battle ground.

Jack's clothes were all ready ready for the hills; don't forget he was in the body of Trom who was dressed appropriately and he came with all his strengths too. Trom was born for hill walking; he was after all a Clurichaun and a member of the Family Hawksbeard, the greatest hunters of them all.

Pulling the cape tightly over his shoulders and fastening the silver brooch, of the tree in the tree, onto the front reminded Jack of his first outing. He didn't know what to expect that time when everything he confronted was so new and amazing. However this was different, he might not know the paths he would be walking on but now he had some idea of the dark forces he might meet. And he wasn't stupid. Cobs had just given off to him for something he didn't even remember doing and he began to find himself doing things that seemed natural but on second thoughts they were not things he normally would do. Were they things Trom did? Sometimes he could feel himself slipping a little further away as if going down a rabbit hole with no possibility of return and it took all his concentration to make the body he occupied move and talk at the same time. Other times it became natural and he didn't give it a second thought. He knew the Talisman was working but maybe it was working too well.

Was time running out?

"I'll have to make an excuse to my father why we are going into the hills," explained Cobs. "He is sure to want to come. If we try and sneak out he'll know something is wrong and come after us. He is the best tracker in all of Ireland and he can smell a lie a mile away."

"Then let me do the talking," said Jack. "I have the perfect excuse to go into the hills and when he hears it he will understand."

With backpacks filled, suitable clothing adorned, the three explorers set off. Within moments they came to a stop; their first major obstacle to overcome.

"I will not," shouted the Dullahan.

"Oh go on, you know you want to," taunted Cobs.

"I do not want to," the Dullahan shouted even louder. Jack sensed his pride might have something to do with it.

"Oh yes you do," said Jack. He was joining Cobs in making gentle fun of the Dullahan. They were all standing at the top of the Curraghard helter skelter-staircase and they were trying to make the Dullahan go down the slide that encased it. After the umpteenth taunt from Jack and Cobs he gave in.

"I am just glad my head can't see what I'm about to dooooooooo."

The sight of a headless horseman sliding as fast as the wind down a helter skelter is not something Jack saw every day but the sound of his laughter was a rare treat. For one brief moment Jack forgot the perilous quest he was about to embark on and the fact that he might not return. No one knew this better than Jack for he had half an idea what waited if his plan worked.

Outside the Curraghard tree stood Poitin and Blaithnaid. They had spent the morning like most parents after a party; cleaning up. When the three adventurers spilled off the end of the slide and fell out through the front door, they had to explain themselves very quickly. They remembered that Jack said he would do all the talking.

"Father, Mother. I have a small confession." Jack kept his eyes to the ground; he knew they would give him away, his eyes looking out Trom's face. "I have left something up in the hills and I want to go and get it right now. Cobs and the Dullahan are joining me."

Poitin spoke. "We'll join you Trom. I'd like nothing better than a good walk into the hills."

"No father, truth is... well...it's not exactly a something I forgot, it's more of a someone and she's kind of shy you see," said Jack. He impressed himself at how good he had become at lying.

"Ahhh. I see. Well then you'd better hurry on hadn't you. It's been a long time. I only hope she waited for you Trom. A century might not be a long time but the heart can be a fickle thing. Isn't that right Blaithnaid?"

Blaithnaid just threw her eyes up and sighed. "Don't listen to him son. If she knows how wonderful you are as much as I do then I know she'll have waited. I've things in the larder older than a hundred years; sure it's no time at all. Jack made a mental note that if they returned he would not be eating anything from the Hawksbeard larder without checking with Cobs how old it was first.

Jack peeked up slightly at Blaithnaid as she spoke. Her words were full of kindness just like those of his own mother. As soon as the thought of his mother Martha flashed across his mind, he had a bad feeling, a sense of foreboding, but he shook it off, convincing himself he was just being silly.

They set off in the early afternoon sun heading directly toward one of the greatest mountains in all of Ireland, Slieve Donard. The walk was pleasant for the air was clear and the views of the sea as they climbed higher were breathtaking. It never ceased to amaze Jack that no matter how many times he walked the pathways in the Mournes it was always like the first time. The colours changed not only with the seasons but also with each passing cloud. The sun would break through from above and light up a patch of hillside or reflect off a flowing stream and give the place a whole new feeling.

The smells of heather and damp grass lifted into the air with each crunch of gravel underfoot. But the sounds of the Mournes filled Jack's thoughts completely and it was well that they did for the real reason they were heading towards Slieve Donard scared him immensely. The trail up into the hills was long and difficult but the Dullahan reminded them that they would be going beyond the wall for the Silver Orb no longer existed. They were free to roam and explore every new part of the Mourne Mountains marked out on Cob's map. But little did Jack think where he was now heading was the last place on earth he would have ever have expected.

"I don't like this one bit Jack," said Cobs. "What you are about to attempt has never been done before. I don't even think it is possible."

Jack pretended not to hear Cobs and he kept walking. He moved just in front of the Dullahan to place a physical barrier between himself and Cobs.

"I don't care where you move to Jack Turner I still don't like this. Since we left the Curraghard Tree all I keep seeing is solitary magpies. It's as if they know something and you know what they say Jack.

"Yes I do, when it comes to magpies, everyone does," replied Jack. "One for sorrow. Two for joy... But my mother always told me if you say 'Hello Mr. Magpie,' when you see one on their own you will be fine."

"Well I still think you should reconsider," said Cobs.

But nothing was going to make Jack reconsider. He had made his mind up. He was about to raise something from the grave.

Chapter 22

Run

Long tendrils of flame swept over the rafters and swooped down the walls of the living room. The scorching heat hissed as the fire took hold of the cottage. It moved like a living raging creature that roared as it moved. The fire's destructive path led to the floor where Martha still lay unconscious. Her face glowed crimson from the strong glare of the fire but still she didn't budge. Soon the smoke would overwhelm her and then it would seek out Matthew and he too would perish.

Smoke billowed out through the front of the cottage, where the door no longer stood, and spewed into the air. The smell soon attracted the attention of all the villagers of Springwell and they looked to the hillside and saw the cottage in flames against the night sky.

The first man arrived at the doorway within minutes. He was a friend of the Turners, a local fisherman, David Burns. He stood at the doorway and shouted inside. "Martha, Matthew are you in there?" He heard a groan from inside so, without a moment's thought for his own safety, he ran straight through the plumes of smoke. Once inside he quickly made out the figure of Martha lying on the floor. He ran to her aid, picked her up, slung her over his shoulder, and ran to the safety of the garden. The fresh air helped to stir her and she opened her eyes and looked back to her beloved home. Her eyes were wide with fear and she screamed.

With the fire demanding everyone's immediate and undivided attention no one except Martha noticed the dark unnatural cloud passing them by as they ran to the cottage to put out the flames. Martha had to decide, to chase after Doolen or save her husband.

"Matthew's in there. You have to go back and get him."

"The smoke's too thick now. It's not safe," said David.

"But he's at the back of the cottage, in his room," said Martha.

"There's no way he'll survive in there and I must save Jack."

"Is Jack in there too?" asked David.

Martha knew she couldn't explain what was going on. She had to do something. But what?

"You must stay here Martha. There's no going back in now."

By now, a huge crowd had gathered and they had already started filling buckets of water from the well at the side of the cottage. Hand over hand they passed them to one another forming a chain from the water supply right to the door of the cottage.

Martha ignored David and got to her feet. She was unsteady at first but she stumbled over to one of the buckets of water as it passed her and soaked her handkerchief. Then ignoring the pleas of everyone who watched she ran straight back into the cottage.

The acrid stench hit her hard and she fell immediately to her knees and it was this that saved her for the air was breathable here. She crawled along the earthen floor ignoring the searing pain on her back from the intense heat as the lit thatch dropped in clumps to the ground. It hampered her pathway but still she crept forward. The shouts of the villagers merged with the crackling and sputtering of the flames all around her but all she could focus on was her husband's voice. She knew he lay unconscious but she imagined him calling to her, beckoning her to him.

Hisses of steam burst around her as some of the buckets of water found their way to the flames, dousing them on contact. She could see the open door of her bedroom and she edged towards it. The smoke was so thick now and all she wanted to do was rest, but Matthew's voice grew louder in her mind. She breeched the threshold and found Matthew lying defenceless. With every ounce of strength she could muster she attempted to lift Matthew but he was a hulk of a man.

There had to be another way. The room was heavy with smoke with no visibility but Martha instinctively knew her way around it. The tiny window was just to her right. Not big enough to escape by but enough if she could only get Matthew to it to draw breath. She willed herself to crawl along the wall until she found what she was looking for; the tiny stool. With all her might she flung it and smiled when she heard the sound of breaking glass. Fresh air rushed into the room and she edged nearer to it. She knew it would feed the flames once it reached them but it was her only chance. She got to the window and shouted.

"Help...Help. We're round here. Hurry..."

149

Over the sound of the fire her voice was drowned out. No one was coming to their rescue. But Martha wasn't about to give up. She went back to the bed and grabbed the quilt with Matthew upon it. She slung the edge of the quilt over her shoulder and leaned forward, dragging Matthew inch by inch away from the flames now licking at the doorway to their bedroom. She inched painfully over to the window and once she had Matthew there she dragged his body up to the hole in the glass. She could hear him breathe in the air.

Now she was at the mercy of the fire. Would it consume them both and leave her son alone in the world? She screamed again until her throat was about to burst but this time someone did hear her pleas. The villagers came to the side of the cottage and leapt up onto the thatch and began to bash and kick it in. With a hole just wide enough they were able to hoist Martha and Matthew to safety. The cottage was consumed by smoke that would have surely killed the inhabitants but luckily and thanks to the valiant efforts of the village folk the flames were soon put under control and the fire was contained to the living area. Within the hour it was out.

Jack lay oblivious to everything that was happening around him. He was high up in the attic of the Old Mill and nothing would disturb him there. His mind was elsewhere on a serious quest but his time was growing short. It wouldn't be long before the Talisman gave up his position. Doolen had a sense of the object but for some reason something blocked her from seeing it.

Martha had coughed until her ribs ached but still her only concern was Matthew and Jack. She didn't exactly know where Jack was but she was certain he had not been in the cottage when the fire broke out. She asked the villagers to take care of her husband and they assured her they would. With great difficulty she managed to get to her feet. She couldn't tell anyone what she had just witnessed for she knew the story to be too incredible. She looked down the hillside that overlooked Springwell Port and tried to imagine where her son might be and then she looked down at her frail husband lying on the ground, his breathing so shallow she thought it would stop at any moment. What could she do?

----------------------*---------------------

The Old Hag Doolen was searching for her prey, stalking it like a cat would a mouse. And when she caught it she would toy with it for a while then devour it whole.

Chapter 23

Old Battleground

The route from the Curraghard Tree into the mountains was an especially beautiful one.

"This is the Spinkwee River Jack and up ahead is the Pot of Legawherry," said Cobs. "Is it not the most beautiful of sights? See the pinnacles of granite. That's where we're headed."

After several hours of trekking over the rough heather Jack's muscles began to cramp and he decided to sit down. The others were glad, for without wanting to admit it, they too were feeling a little drained. But they were now on the back of Commadagh Mountain and the views over the surrounding area, back out to sea with the soft forest-fringed lines blending into the distant beaches were dramatic and a magical atmosphere that only exists in the Mournes settled around them.

Cobs looked at Jack but instead of seeing his face full of wonder at the amazing sights he could see a face full of angst.

"Do ya know Jack there's nothing so bad that it couldn't be worse."

"What?"

"You shouldn't dread the winter till there's snow on your blanket."

"What are you talking about Cobs?" said Jack, his tone unusually sharp. He drummed ferociously on his knees as he spoke.

"All I'm trying to tell you is not to worry. We're all in this together and you need to know that." Jack just stared out into the distance and rocked back and forth. Cobs put his arm around Jack's shoulder to try and comfort him.

They set off again and soon they had reached the Mighty Mourne Wall and the walking party came to a stop. They were in full view of several sculpted pillars of rock facing southwards over the rest of the Mournes.

Jack put his hand over the wall and laughed each time when he wasn't hit by a bolt of energy. The Silver Orb had been shattered and it was all thanks to him. But he could not rest on his laurels for he had an even greater task at hand.

"Jack my map calls these weathered pillars the Eternal Sentinals."

Jack felt they were watching him with their protective eyes. The three friends carried on over murmuring streams and twisting paths until they reached the top of Slieve Commedagh but they didn't stop to rest. They marched straight on along the Mourne Wall all the way to Slieve Donard. When they reached its summit they stood side by side and looked out to where the Shimna River met the sea. From their great vantage point high upon the back of the king of all mountains, they could see the mighty Mourne Wall stretch on for miles. It hugged the contours of the hills and valleys and seemed in perfect harmony with its surroundings. The wall impressed Jack every time he saw it. The workmanship was incredible. The Elderfolk were master craftsmen, cutting and shaping the granite rock into a thing of beauty.

The Dullahan pointed down the mountainside into what was once the Inner Realm.

"I have taken us this way to show you all that is at stake," said the Dullahan. Jack could see the forest below. That was their destination. He looked at Cobs and smiled but Cobs could see the fear in his eyes. He tugged on his tall hat in a gesture of reassurance and winked.

"It'll be fine lad," said Cobs.

"Why of course it'll be fine," bellowed the Dullahan. "A man of your cunning and ingenuity can move mountains if he sets his mind to it."

"My father told me he has never met a braver person in all the lands than you Jack Turner," added Cobs.

The words gave temporary comfort but then Jack was sure he spied what they were searching for. It was only a speck far out in the distance and a chill ran down his spine. But he couldn't go back. He could never return to his own body knowing he hadn't tried.

"I think lunch is in order. I don't know about you two but I'm starving," said Cobs already sitting cross-legged on a rock opening his pack. "I don't mean to be rude but do you eat?" he asked the Dullahan. The Dullahan did not reply but Cobs swore he could hear him chuckle.

"I think I'm hungry," said Jack. "It's hard to tell. I mean I can't remember the last time that Trom ate. I filled up before I went to sleep back in the mill."

"It'll do no harm then Jack. Fill him up with all the things you like. I've brought half the larder with me. Jack quickly remembered Blaithnaid saying about having food in there as old as one hundred years but since it wasn't his very own stomach but really Troms he didn't ask questions about the food.

Jack glanced to the Dullahan and then to Cobs. He was happy to be in their company but still the enormity of what lay ahead weighed heavy on his shoulders. A year ago he was a boy without a care in the world, now he was about to do something that had never been done before and it frightened him. His mixed feelings made him feel guilty and he fought to suppress them.

After a feed of incredible apple pie, Cobs had definitely packed it especially for Jack or so he thought, they headed on. Heading down the side of Rocky Mountain should have been easier than the climb up Donard but with every step, the tiny speck in the distance grew bigger and Jack grew more restless. They crossed over barren shale and through a deserted ruin of a village. The Dullahan explained they belonged to the Booley Folk but they had long since taken to the caves in the mountains when the Shimnavore ravaged the lands.   Only small circular mounds of grassy earth and the odd rough dry stone wall gave away the fact that they were ever there. Soon they reached the edge of the great forest and Jack knew they hadn't far to go. There was no backing out now. It was a good plan, a brave plan but one that Jack wished he had kept to himself. The others had tried to convince him of the danger involved and of the madness at attempting to do such a thing. But both Cobs and the Dullahan agreed that for a father they would do anything.

"It's over there. Look," shouted Cobs walking ahead a good few paces. That's when Jack saw it clearly. It lay in exactly the same place he had left it after the Battle of Annalong Wood, a monstrous corpse that still gave off a horrendous stink so bad that not even the flies would land on it. Jack could smell it even from where he stood…

…Burnt seaweed.

The Shimnavore lay where it had been slain.

Now came the moment of truth. As Jack drew nearer, a fear grew inside him. His heart began to beat faster and his palms began to sweat. He didn't think Trom's body would react in such a way but it responded in exactly the same way as Jack would have in his own. But there was a twitch and a tic thrown in and that most certainly wasn't a trait of Jack's. It had been many hours since Jack took over Trom's body. He knew it wouldn't be for much longer though and the thought of what would happen next was terrifying.

"You know you don't have to go through with this Jack," said Cobs. "I thought you were mad when you explained your plan to us."

Jack could see just how scared Cobs was now that he too confronted the enormous creature.

"I must do it. I cannot think of what might happen. All I know is that I must save my father. I would die on the inside if I left here knowing I was a coward. Now just tell me what I must do," said Jack.

He stared at the Shimnavore's body lying on the heather. This same hulking mass had killed him only days before but it seemed like a lifetime ago. Jack almost had pity for the creature. It had been bred to be evil, to do the bidding of The Old Ones, the Ancients. It was in the nature of the Shimnavore to kill. It wasn't their fault. Jack shook his head; he couldn't believe he was entertaining such thoughts. The thing was a killer and no pity should be cast upon it.

Cobs walked over to Jack and took him by the hand. Together they approached the Shimnavore and Cobs placed Jack's hands on either side of its gigantic muzzle. It repulsed Jack and he flinched at the feel of the slimy, cold skin on his hands. He was grateful though that the hands were actually Troms but it didn't make him feel any less uncomfortable.

"Now Jack. This is not like the last time. All you and Trom had to do was share the same thought and your minds became one and that allowed you to control him. This creature is dead and what's worse it never had a soul so there is no sharing to be done. I know your soul is back in your body in the Outer Realm but I don't know what'll happen when..."

Jack looked up at the Dullahan. He interrupted Cobs. He couldn't listen any longer. He knew what Cobs was saying was true but it didn't help.

"Wish me luck," said Jack.

"Good luck Jack. I know you can do it," said the Dullahan.

Jack looked back at the huge head in front of him. He tried to clear his mind but the sight of his father lying on his bed so close to death would not leave him. Then he suddenly realised that was the answer. He would not clear his mind, he would fill it with all the reasons he had come here today and with all those images in his mind he would be stronger. He thought of his mother, his Nanna Tess, his brother Edmund and of all the new and wonderful creatures he had encountered. Then he focused on one memory, one thing that would never leave him, the eyes that stared at him just before his own life was taken. The eyes... the soulless eyes of the Shimnavore.

Something strange began to happen. The rabbit hole Jack felt he was falling down suddenly widened and a great black chasm lay below him. He teetered on the brink and the edges were beginning to crumble until he no longer could find purchase. Then it happened- he was falling, falling deeper and deeper into the abyss. Darkness surrounded him but fleeting images smashed into his mind. They were memories, but they were not his, nor were they Trom's. Jack realised he was glimpsing fragments of the Shimnavore's life.

A scalding surge of heat exploded through his body and he knew the tears he had thrown into the Shimnavore's eyes caused it. It was the only weak spot. The Ancients may have created the Shimnavore but they were still born in the River Shimna. Its eyes were closed when they arrived into the world. Jack could sense this and he knew that when the creature had opened them it was too late. The water's powers had made every part of the Shimnavore invulnerable but it never washed over the eyes.

Then Jack could see hordes of the beasts, the stench did not seem so awful now, it was almost strangely familiar and comforting. Jack watched as images of a terrible war waged with the Elderfolk. He felt the pain and isolation of being cast into the Orb and the hunger than never left him. A creature that could not be satisfied. But there it was. Jack knew instantly when he saw his master. A creature to rule all creatures but it was only a faint and fading image. Just as Jack was about to focus on its face a blast of light struck him.

The Shimnavore opened its eyes.

Chapter 24

The Search

Martha barely had a chance to collect her thoughts before she spied a dark shadow in the distance. A reek of stale breath followed in its wake and Martha recognised it immediately. It was the Hag Doolen heading down to the pier. She kept a close watch on her and made sure she couldn't be seen. At least she hoped she couldn't be seen. The creature that scurried over the ground ahead of her had no eyes. Had she not witnessed Doolen in her cottage half-human/ half-scuttling swarm of insects that should have been her feet she would have thought herself crazed. But how would she confront such a creature. Martha had experienced first hand the strength that belied the Hag's fragile frame. What would she do if she caught up with her? How would she defend her son from such a being? There was no one she could turn to for help and she knew she could never last up against such a foe but she had to try.

The cloud of insects moved faster as they approached the shore. Martha hid behind a nearby tree and looked over towards the pier in the harbour, her heart in her mouth. But to her delight Jack wasn't sitting on the end of it as she had feared. Now she knew where he was, the only other place she knew he felt safe...

Martha turned to leave; she no longer cared what the Hag was doing, all she wanted was to be at her son's side. Her mother's instinct told her that he needed her.

Something did not feel right and she would try anything to help her son. She turned to run and a branch broke under her foot. She froze on the spot.

At the water's edge the great swarm of insects rose high into the air. Martha could see them lifting high above the harbour. She hoped with all her heart that they could not see her. She didn't move a muscle and she held her breath until her eyes began to water. The insect-swarm crossed over the harbour and headed towards the cemetery. Now was her chance and she took it. Lifting her long dress, she sprinted up towards the Old Mill. She tried the main doors but they were bolted shut. Next, she tried around the side and came across the same small flour shoot Jack had but it too was locked. Martha knew her boy was hiding inside. Now all she had to do was get the key from Davy Evans the mill house owner and she knew where he would be at this hour, in Henry Kirk's tavern on the other side of the village.

Meanwhile, Jack still lay among the dry straw high up in the attic of the old mill. The honey he had eaten in such vast quantities seemed to be working for he had a boundless energy, all be it trapped inside his sleeping body. The Talisman on the back of his neck glowed but its light could not be seen to give away his position and Jack's mind was a world away facing demons of its own. He continued to sleep fitfully unaware of the horrors that were occurring in his own realm, the horrors his mother was facing on her own.

The Old Hag had taken solid form again right at the steps of her tomb. She looked down into the familiar darkness past the broken tombstone and tried to see if anything stirred below. Nothing did. Somehow, she thought Jack might have returned to her tomb. She had hoped it would be that easy. She knew he was drawn to her, she sensed it the day they met, almost as if they were kindred spirits.   Doolen knew he had been searching for something he could use against her. Instinctively she went to the shelf where the useless piece of Talisman sat and she noticed the thick layer of dust had been disturbed. Small fingerprints imbedded in the grime gave Jack away. Doolen's head bent backwards, her mouth opened, and she wailed, "Jack Turner, I will find you." Her haunting voice carried up the hillside and one petrified mother heard it as she entered the Hermitage Tavern looking for Davy Evans

Henry Kirk was a man of tradition. He liked his dinner to be served on time, his supper to be one hour before bedtime but most of all he didn't and would never allow a woman to enter his pub. Remember this is 1847, and things were very different then. Martha saw Evans propping up the corner of the bar and she called to him.

"Mr Evans I need your key to the mill. My son Jack is in grave danger and I think he is in there hiding."

"Get out of here woman," shouted Kirk and he pointed at the door. "Get out now."

"I will leave once I have the key," said Martha.

Mr Evans crossed the room and grabbed Martha by the wrist. He turned and began to drag her out.

A rage grew in Martha. No man would ever tell her what to do and no man would ever lay a finger on her. In all her years with Matthew he had never once spoken to her like that and she certainly wasn't going to take it from this buffoon.

Martha practically snarled at Evans, "If you know what's good for me you'll give me that key." She turned to Kirk and continued, "And as for you don't ever speak to me like that again do you hear me? Now let me go."

Kirk had never heard a woman speak like this before and it frightened him.

"I will not."

Martha knew words were of no further use. She lifted her boot and sent her heel crashing down on top of Kirk's foot. He instantly let her go and fell to the floor in agony. She ran over to Evans and grabbed him by the scruff of his neck.

"Key. Now." It was all she needed to say. Evans thrust the key into her palm. "Times are changing gentlemen. Best get used to it."

She slammed the door after her and was gone.

Chapter 25

Untravelled Road

Jack's eyes slowly grew accustomed to his surroundings. The sky was beginning to darken but he could still see the trees of Annalong Wood and up the hill where he knew the opening of the Percy Byshee Cave lay. However, something was amiss. He was alone. His friends had abandoned him. He went to speak but instead of words coming out of his mouth, a roar emanated from his throat.

Down the hill, hidden safely behind the trees, cowered a Clurichaun and, trying to pretend he only followed the tiny fellow to protect him, sat the Dullahan. As soon as the Shimnavore began to stir they both took flight. They were afraid something might have gone wrong and their instincts kicked in. From where they hid they could see the mighty body of the Shimnavore standing up on its hind legs. Its telescopic neck lengthened and the huge muzzle tilted to one side. Then two enormous claws went into the air, palms facing upwards and Cobs recognised the same sarcastic gesture he had seen the squirrel had made when Jack had taken over its body.

"He's done it," shouted Cobs grabbing the Dullahan by the coat tails and dancing a merry gig.

"I believe you are right," said the Dullahan. "That boy is like nothing I have ever seen. Not in all my lifetimes. And I know there is still more to him than even he is aware."

The two cowardly friends stepped out of the tree line and shouted up the valley towards Jack.

Jack tried to take a step forward but he couldn't see where he was going. He stumbled and fell into the marshy ground spitting huge mouthfuls of dirt past his many rows of fangs as he tried to get up. He could not understand how he was staring up at the clouds yet his mouth was beneath the dirt with a worm making its way past his incisors. Everything was the wrong way round. It was just like the time he pretended to shave in the mirror. He had taken his father's shaving soap, made a huge lather, and put it on his cheeks and chin. Then he took the cutthroat razor and proceeded to shave his pretend beard. The first drop of blood let him know he'd done something wrong. The small round mirror over the basin had cheated. When he went to move one way his hand had moved in the opposite direction.

Something was not quite right and the body he had entered was topsy-turvy and backside about face. Then he remembered. No wonder he couldn't move in the regular way. The Shimnavore had eyes in the back of its head and moving forward meant travelling backwards. This would take some getting used to. Jack looked down and a huge long rugged spine spread out before him. He could see two huge flanks jutting out at the base of his back and the tail with its trident fork dug into the earth.

Jack began to laugh uncontrollably. Being in a body with such, immense power filled him so many mixed emotions but the one that surfaced the most was joy. Never in his life had he felt so strong, so invincible and it was good. A feeling he could get very used to. But something was missing, something intangible but something vital. What was it? It worried him.

Trom trembled on the ground looking up at the wretched creature. The last thing he remembered was sitting in his father's study thinking about the Shimna River. Now he waited for his untimely death. The hulking great mass towered over him roaring into his face. He had only heard of the Shimnavore from old legends and he saw the last one die in Annalong wood, killed by Jack Turner. He looked all about him trying to get his bearings. He saw the tree line, the cave high in the hills and he recognised the view down the valley. He was in Annalong Wood and the dead Shimnavore had risen from the dead. Jack had not killed him after all and now it would exact its revenge on him. He knew better than to try and run so he closed his eyes and waited for death. It might be a coward's way out but he really didn't want to see what was coming next.

"You did it my young man," shouted Cobs approaching the Shimnavore gingerly. "Tell me you did it."

The Shimnavore went to agree but the words Jack tried to form would not come out of his mouth. Instead more guttural roars came from with the cavernous mouth of the creature. Jack could not understand why he couldn't get the thing to talk properly.

Trom half-opened his left eye and the scene before him beggared belief. His tiny brother Cobs was in full conversation with the deadliest and most evil creature the

InBetween had ever witnessed. He had no clue what had happened since he agreed to Jack taking over his body. But he could sense a tiny part Jack was still with him even though he no longer had control over him. He had flashes of Jack's memory lingering in his mind too; beautiful snap shots of a brother, a loving mother, a strong and loving father. He could feel the warmth that he knew Jack felt when he thought of him and he understood the bond they both shared. No wonder this small human would go to any lengths to save him. But Trom still couldn't figure out why he hadn't become a feast for the Shimnavore. Then he heard Cobs speak and it all made sense.

"Jack calm down," shouted Cobs. Sure it's a small miracle that you were able to take over a Shimnavore in the first place. Be grateful for that alone. I mean, not only was the bloomin' creature soulless, it was dead for goodness sake. Give it a few minutes until you get accustomed to the husk you're inside."

The Shimnavore nodded knowingly and Trom stood up, suddenly realising what had happened. He went to shake Jack's new hand but Cobs quickly stopped him.

"I wouldn't do that if I was you brother. I know Jack is inside there but I don't know if the Shimnavore could still age you one hundred years if you touch it. I know it wouldn't kill you but a hundred years is a hundred years in anyone's eyes."

The Dullahan agreed but grabbed hold of the Shimnavore's claw anyway. He didn't feel any different. Yes, a hundred years to him would be insignificant given his time on the earth but he still would have noticed something.

"I think it's alright. That particular power the Shimnavore once held seems to have gone when it died and thankfully it hasn't come back."

On hearing that Cobs leapt into the air and put both his arms around the Shimnavore's neck. He hugged him with all his might.

"You're unbelievable Jack Turner. There is truly nothing you can't do once you set your mind to it. It must be the Elderfolk's blood in ya."

The Dullahan just tutted when he heard the mention of the Elderfolk.

"Trom," said Cobs. "Can I introduce you to Jack Turner, a creature so feared that the mere mention of his name strikes fear into his enemy's hearts. Or at least it will now once they see him."

Trom laughed and extended his hand again. He watched in awe, tinged with just the right amount of fear, as Jack's claws enveloped his tiny hand.

"Pleased to meet you Trom," laughed Jack and this time the words that came past his enormous fangs made sense. They may have sounded like a giant bear trying to talk for the first time but Jack had found his voice none the less.

"See I told you Jack. Patience is the best virtue," said Cobs. He fidgeted as he spoke and Jack couldn't help but notice.

"Is everything all right?" he asked.

"If truth be told Jack I'm worried. I'm worried time is fast running out for you. You were in Trom for quite some time and now you have jumped straight into this creature. The longer you stay outside your own body the harder it might be to return and the temptation to remain in the body of something this powerful might be too great. Salix had stayed in Tiernan Speedwell, the Bogbean's body, because it became so seductive to remain there and you could come to the same end. If you grow too accustomed to the power you now feel it might entice you never to want to leave. Time is of the essence."

The Shimnavore's mighty head leaned down and nuzzled the tiny Clurichaun. Jack knew his friend was right and he wanted him to know he was grateful for his concern.

"Jack, you must go now," ordered the Dullahan. "You know the next part of the journey must be done alone. We cannot go with you, much as we'd like to but no creature with a soul can cross the Devil's Coachroad. It would break the spell put on it by the Elderfolk and would be the end to everything as we know it. Blianta told me that if any creature dared to try not only would it mean certain death and damnation for the traveller it would awaken the All-Seer. No one in all my time trapped inside the Silver Orb dared to see if it were true. The Evil spirits I have lived with are a very superstitious lot. The Shimnavore were enough to contend with but knowing there was something more powerful and even more dangerous locked away in the hills was enough to scare anyone away."

"Who is the All-Seer?" asked Jack, his booming voice echoing out across the hills.

"No one knows Jack," replied the Dullahan. "All Blianta told me was that you do not want to wake him. Even the Elderfold were afraid when they unearthed him. Of all the creatures they found running amok when they arrived the All-Seer seemed to rule over all the others. A hidden master if you will. The night creatures did its bidding even though it slept. The Elderfolk sensed its power and they knew it was the one thing in the entire universe capable of capturing the soul of an Elderfolk. It is why they chose to build the Mourne Wall where they did. They also left the All-Seer sleeping where they found it but they bound the area with a powerful spell at the end of the Devil's Coachroad, a path in the Mournes never to be walked with body and soul combined. Now you must walk it if you are to find your father's soul."

Jack looked up the valley and could see the path he had to take. Cobs, the Dullahan and Trom walked with the gigantic beast but no one spoke. Words did not seem appropriate at such a time. At the foot of the Coachroad they all could see the steep path leading upwards and ahead of them.

A fine mist began to descend on the hills and Jack had the terrible feeling a storm was coming.

Chapter 26

True Hero

As promised after the fire, Matthew had been lifted to the safety of his friend David Burns' small cottage where he lay on a soft bed, wrapped in the owner's finest patchwork quilt. David and several of the villagers, who helped carry Matthew, sat outside his bedroom. David reached high up on the shelf and lifted down a bottle of whiskey and filled several wee glasses.

"I want to raise a toast to the finest man ever to walk in Springwell. He may be a quiet man but every resident has something to be grateful to him for," said David.

"I know. He saw the hole in my thatched roof after that winter storm a few years back. However, come morning the hole had been patched. I tried to thank him but he was having none of it. He told me Mia, the fearless Queen of the Faeries, must have done it," said Old Mr McGladdery and he raised his glass. "May the good Lord taking a liking to you Matthew Turner... But not too soon!"

Everyone nodded in agreement and raised their glasses.

"My flock of sheep definitely had help finding their own way home the night of the great rains and when I saw Matthew walking down my lane from my fields he said he was just out for a stroll, "said Brian Cullen, a local farmer. He raised his glass. "May the hinges of our friendship never grow rusty."

Everyone raised their glassed again.

"He exhibited extraordinary strength when he lifted the boat that had fallen over on me as I mended a crack in the keel. He just picked it up, with the strength of ten men and freed me. As soon as more help came, he just walked off quietly, "said Oisin Kennedy, another fisherman. "May bad fortune follow you the rest of your life... but never catch up."

More residents of Springwell gathered around David Burns' door and began to tell stories of the man. It was only when they shared their tales that they realised how truly wonderful a member of the community Matthew was. One person did not know the lengths Matthew had gone to for the other.

It sometimes takes the worst thing to happen to know how much you are respected and needed but most of all loved.

Inside, lying in his bed, the unconscious Matthew could sense footsteps. Something was coming- something terrible. The footfalls were heavy, they were distant, but they were coming. But for some strange reason Matthew welcomed the horrible thing that drew closer and with every step it filled him with hope. The trap that grew all around him, suffocating his spirit seemed for just a moment to weaken. Matthew could glimpse into the darkness and make out the shape of a cavern. He could feel the weight of a mountain above him but still he felt something. A feeling, an emotion.For the first time in what seemed like forever emotions were feeding his spirit, not draining them until he thought the very end was just a heartbeat away. The smell of burning seaweed filled the air and the rancid, putrid odour strangely filled him with a

sense of comfort. All he had to do was hang on. It wouldn't
be much longer.

Chapter 27

The Devil's Coachroad

The fine mist quickly turned to rain and thick sheets began to fall on the valley. The clouds overhead had gathered almost in defence of the path Jack was about to cross. It soon became a river but the advantage of having massive claws to walk on helped. Jack got used to walking backwards, the best thing to do was not to think too much about it, let it come naturally. But there was certainly nothing natural about a boy-inhabited-Shimnavore walking jerkily up a mountainside. The sight would have scared a Banshee.

Jack came to abrupt stop. He stood at the bottom of the Devil's Coachroad. It was a treacherous scree-scarred chasm with cascading waterfalls that flowed down through the huge gully. A more unwelcoming sight he could not have imagined. It reached high up into the mountainside and Jack was grateful he controlled a body that could cope with such an arduous task. He knew in his own form he certainly couldn't. Never in his wildest dreams did he ever think he would be grateful for living inside the dead husk of such an abomination. Having no soul helped as well. He hoped his was safe and well back in his body. He hadn't thought too much about that part when he leapt into the Shimnavore. His judgement had been clouded by the loyalty to his father but he wouldn't change a thing even if he had to decide again.

"Are ya certain ya want to go through with this?" asked Cobs, not too sure if he really wanted an answer.

"I'm afraid so Cobs." The Shimnavore knelt down beside his tiny companion and their eyes met. "Will you wait for me till I come back?" Jack looked uncertain of his return and Cobs knew it.

"We'll all be waiting won't we?" said Cobs. Trom and the Dullahan agreed. "Now be off with ya before we change our minds." Cobs laughed trying to hide his fear and give his best friend some reassurance.

Jack began his ascent and he welcomed the feel of the rain on his face, well the back of his head anyway. It was all terribly confusing. He watched as his claws gripped the earth beneath him and tore up sods of turf with every step. Higher and higher he climbed but he stumbled on the broken rocks and a pain shot through his leg. Then he suddenly realised, just not aging anyone a hundred years, when he touched them, he wasn't invulnerable like the Shimnavore. Jack had some of the Strength of the Shimnavore but most of it was just for show. He wouldn't last a second against a real Shimnavore but thankfully that was not a problem as they were extinct. He was the last of the Shimnavore, well in body at least.

He also knew of the curse on the Coachroad and he hoped that whatever watched over it could not see the gash on his leg. Being dead had one advantage the deep wound was not bleeding. No heart pumped in this husk of a body, no heat could be felt or cold for that matter. The body was one of the walking dead but this didn't upset Jack in the least. It served his purpose well.

He inched his way up the cliffside and the brutal winds whipped all around him. Great walls of granite began to close in on him and when he turned to look back down the valley, he was met with shards of rain pelting into his eyes. He tried to ignore the pain in his leg but he had no choice but to rest. He slumped down onto a patch of heather and breathed heavily. The Coachroad was aptly named he thought but he wondered where it led. So far all he could see were rocks and rare patches of vegetation. The ground had been undisturbed and no traces of any animals were apparent anywhere.

He looked into the distance and spied a tight 'v' shape in the rocks at the top of the mountain. But there was something more - something that was there and not there all at the same time. Jack couldn't quite place it but he knew he had had the same feeling once before. Then it came to him - in front of Pierce's Castle. He remembered seeing only rocks until he crossed his eyes as Cobs had instructed and then the castle appeared out of thin air. There was no way it could work again he thought but it was worth a try. He remembered back to the first time he blew on the dandelion. He was convinced there was no way his wish could come true but a tiny part hoped it just might. With the same hope, he crossed his eyes. Nothing happened. He tried again and again. Then something caught his eye. Something dark... a shadow that wasn't there before - a darkness on the side of the mountain. Could it be an opening? Yes. Jack convinced himself that he saw a crag just below the shadow. He rose to his feet and with a renewed vigour scaled the rough granite until he reached the outcrop of rock jutting out just above his head. He reached up and searched for a finger-hold or in this case a claw-hold. He found one and pulled himself up.

Slowly he climbed until he reached his goal. He sat on the ledge of rock and exhaled in relief. A cloud of steam rose from his mouth. He could not see it form for his eyes were on the other side of his head. Now all he had to do was find out where the dark hole in the mountain led. He knew he had no choice but to enter into it.

He glanced once more into the sky.

The storm was so close now.

Chapter 28

Thunder and Lightning

The heavens opened and heavy torrents of rain lashed the village. A deafening roar of thunder boomed out and in an instant a bolt of lightning splintered the sky. Martha urged her feet to move faster as she raced back to the Old Mill with the key of the door held tightly in her hand. The sound of the Old Hag's hellish screams still echoed in her mind. She watched as the storm clouds gathered, almost supernaturally, above her but she pressed on, clinging to the hope that her boy was unharmed.

There's nowhere else he would be. She would often find him there after Edmund died. He said he found comfort in the mill as they often played together in amongst the sacks of flour. It had become his refuge, his fort.

She reached the doors, placed the key into the lock, and turned it hoping her son would be playing among the sacks of flour. To her dismay he wasn't. She looked around. There were no signs of life. Then she noticed something. The giant ladder that ran all the way to the attic was missing. Her boy had to be high up in his castle but why hadn't he come when he heard the door opening. Of course, he would never look over the edge to see who had entered for that would give his position away and he was in hiding. There had to be a way to reach him. There had to be more than one ladder. She raced around the ground floor of the mill and to her utter delight she found another ladder. This one looked like it had not been used in a very long time. Half the rungs were missing and the termites looked like they had been feasting on the rest of it for some time. It creaked and wobbled as she lifted it and placed it onto the rafters above her.

Martha placed her foot on the first rung and put her weight on it. It cracked beneath her and she immediately stomped back to the ground but it didn't stop her, not for a moment. She tried the second rung only this time she tested its strength.

It held.

She rose higher into the mill.

One foot slowly moving over the other.

The ladder began to bow.

She had reached the middle.

She was so high up.

Hand over hand.

Foot over foot.

She was now three quarters the way up.

But the ladder continued to bow.

The more it bowed the less ladder rested against the rafter at the top.

Martha didn't look up; she kept her gaze straight ahead of her.

Only four more rungs to go.

There was less than an inch of the ladder leaning against the beam.

Three rungs to go.

Only half an inch of ladder left resting on the beam.

With the next foot on the rung the ladder suddenly jerked.

Martha fell backward.

She threw up her hands instinctively.

The ladder fell and crashed onto the ground below.

A cloud of dust rose into the air.

Where was Martha?

Luckily for her when her instinct kicked in. She reached out and miraculously managed to catch the edge of the floor of the attic. Three fingers of her left hand gripped on for dear life. She looked down and could see the floor far below. This wasn't her time to die. Her grip tightened and soon her other hand joined the three fingers. With all the might she could muster, she hauled herself onto the high ledge. She just lay there, grateful to be alive.

Now to find Jack.

Chapter 29

Hag

The huge cauldron in the centre of Doolen's tomb bubbled furiously and thick grey plumes of smoke erupted from within. They licked their way over the edge and spilled to the floor spreading outwards forming an eerie mist. Every candle on the walls was lit and sent a haunting glow onto the face of the Old Hag Doolen. She leaned over the cauldron and immersed both hands in the putrid waters.

"Rise up elements of this forsaken earth and do my bidding. Lightening reveal the pathway to the boy I seek and thunder shout out his name. I will not be stopped."

She threw her hands into the air and cackled loudly.

Images of Ireland began to flash up in the water. First it was the whole of Ireland, then it zoomed in and the Mountains of Mourne were visible from the sky and then Springwell Port. But the Hag could see no closer. Something appeared to be blocking her from pinpointing Jack. Thick veins rose up on the side of her forehead and she screamed again. The warts on the side of her nose seemed to grow in size and her eyes grew darker still, if that were at all possible.

The cauldron had worked before in helping her find things. What was blocking it this time? It helped her find Tess when she was a young girl when the Old Hag first came to Annalong. It had been easy to find a tomb and Doolen had been carved over the entrance so she adopted the name. The tomb looked like it hadn't been disturbed for over a hundred years and that part of the cemetery had long since been abandoned. She stayed in Springwell and waited. The spell Tess put on the cottage stopped her from entering or harming anyone who lived there. Doolen knew a strong magic was at work but she couldn't figure out how a human so young could hold such powers.

The Hag reached into the folds of her long ragged robes and took out the pages she had stolen from Tess' room. She could see the page showing the picture of a tree inside a tree. The inner tree had a house on top. It was the Curraghard Tree. The writing on other pages made no sense to her at all but the pictures that accompanied the words told a different story. On one particular page, she could see a pathway running straight up the side of a mountain and at the top a doorway. There were words written underneath but she could not decipher them but the next picture meant she did not have to. It was a rough sketch of an enormous beast and it looked to be sleeping. Surrounding it were other creatures, all dancing around in a circle. She recognised them and shuddered. They were hordes of Shimnavore and they looked as though they dancing around something new and more deadly...

...A giant Shimnavore.

Doolen placed the page into the cauldron's waters and hoped that it might help pinpoint Jack Turner's whereabouts. The cauldron began to glow and the waters inside bubbled even more furiously then they turned black. All the images disappeared. The page did not want to give up its secrets but send a warning to her. She should not be using Elderfolk magic.

Then without warning, the water in cauldron exploded into the air; a massive column of water, as high as the ceiling and inside she could see something. The surface of the water warped and from within a hand pressed hard against the membrane between the air and the water. She leaned in closer and suddenly something tried to reach out and grab her. Then she saw the faces, hundreds of them, and they all looked like they were screaming. The Old Hag's tiny eyes widened for she recognised them. They were the faces of the Elderfolk and the Ancients, The Old Ones. The two enemies were locked together in some sort of chamber. But wait a moment, there was something else in there with them, neither Old Ones nor Elderfolk. It looked human. It was human or half human anyway.

Another face stared in from the other side of the column of water and it had the eyes of Jack Turner but not the body. It had the body of a Shimnavore.

As quickly as the water shot up, it crashed back down, flooded the floor of the tomb, and washed the Old Hag away with it. The force knocked her against one of the walls and the shock was so great it dislodged the red Talisman on the small ledge. It fell onto her lap. A bony hand reached down and picked it up and Doolen roared.

"I will find you Jack Turner, so help me I will, and when I do I'll make you suffer. I will not be defeated by a puny mortal," cried the Old Hag as she rose to her feet. She held the red Talisman in her hands and in a fit of rage she tossed it into her cauldron. She did not expect to see the sights revealed to her. As soon as the Talisman entered the cauldron's waters, it began to glow a brighter shade of red then flashes images beamed onto the ceiling. They were images of other Ancients and Elderfolk and even animals of the Mournes.

Doolen realised that the images projected from the Talisman in the cauldron were things the wearers of Talismans were actually seeing at that very moment or at least it showed their whereabouts. The Old Hag had been privileged to have second sight. To glimpse through the eyes of others. She knew things that had been hidden from her up to now. Doolen now knew Tess had hidden Matthew from her the night of the storm she had conjured. Somehow she was still hiding Jack from her.

However she could not understand how she could be seeing such sights then something suddenly appeared, something trapped in the column of glass she had seen earlier.

It was Matthew Turner.

He faded as fast as he had appeared.

The Talisman was in its dying throes. One final image flashed up. It hovered above the cauldron and the Old Hag grinned from pointed ear to pointed ear. The image was of an old building built on rocks that came right out of the water and rose up to a great height. At the side a wheel churned the stream flowing down into the sea...

...The Old Mill.

The Talisman's last image gave up the whereabouts of the boy she sought. Now she knew where Jack Turner hid and she would take great delight in finding him and taking the Talisman but even better, she would take the greatest delight in taking his life.

"You're mine!" she wailed."AHHHH HA HA HA HA HA."

Chapter 30

Beyond the Darkness

A Shimnavore can see really well in the dark, as good as in daylight, better in fact. But given that this particular Shimnavore had the eyes of Jack Turner the beast stumbled and fell with every step it took. Walking through the hole in the side of the mountain was worrying enough but now Jack was completely blind. He hoped something would happen soon and his eyes would grow accustomed to the darkness. But this wasn't like darkness. This place was devoid of all light as if the very walls were stealing it away, trying to hide something.

Jack closed his eyes for a moment to collect his thoughts and a very strange thing happened. Instead of continued darkness surrounding him he suddenly could make out shapes. The longer he kept his eyes closed the clearer everything became and soon he could make out the outlines of the walls and just up ahead were giant steps leading downwards. Everything had a strange tinge of green about it but he could make out the terrain around him and he saw strange carvings and writings on all the walls. The passageway he was descending seemed to go on forever and as long as he didn't open his eyes he could continue to see clearly. It was like a sixth sense he'd heard people talking about and now he knew firsthand what they meant. He could see without eyes, like a bat when it flies at night. It knows where to go from its echo. Maybe that is how he knew where things were. To be honest Jack did not care he was just glad the Shimnavore's body had not given him away yet.

He carried on into the tunnel not knowing when it would end but he was sure that if he ever got there that there still would be no light. This place made the Lost City under the Valley of Silence seem like a play park for no sound echoed from Jack's footfall and no smell reached his sensitive muzzle.

Jack trudged on for hours as he weaved his way through the mountain following the contours of the rock. He passed over thin narrow paths with bottomless pits on either side just waiting to swallow him up. He dared not look down into them for the temptation to fall in would be too great to bear. He plodded on hoping an echo would sound out and bring comfort to his ears. He hadn't even got a heartbeat to occupy his mind and he knew it was too risky to try whistling his father's tune. But that thought did bring a slight smile to his thick slobbering muzzle. He wondered if a Shimnavore could whistle and he hoped he would live long enough to find out.

Whatever, or whoever, lay ahead Jack knew it would not welcome visitors. He only hoped he would see them before they saw him. He travelled on... always going lower and deeper into the mountain. The air soon grew thick and musky with the tinge of bad breath mixed in. He even felt a warmth coming from up ahead. As he proceeded he came across another entrance way, unlike anything he had seen before. Giant stalagmites and stalactites grew in a great big circle as tall and wide as the Curraghard Tree. Whoever chiselled these out; it must have taken them a thousand lifetimes.

He stopped for a moment at the entrance and a thought struck him, who had carved out all the tunnels he had just come through? In no way did nature do that.

Then without further hesitation, he stepped between two stalagmites. The gap between them must have been about ten feet apart. The ground beneath him suddenly changed from solid granite to a softer more marshy substance but shaped like cobble stones. He welcomed it underfoot.

Jack travelled further into the new section of tunnel. The walls here were nothing like the tunnels he had just come down, these were smooth and lined with a gelatinous substance that felt strange to the touch. They didn't appear to be carved but almost grown, organic even. Every now and then Jack had to step over large undulating curves that were shaped like bones, but he just shook his huge head. Being a Shimnavore gave Jack a newfound confidence, one he was lacking since he had lost his father and part of him didn't want to leave his new body. The only worrying thing was, the part that didn't want to leave seemed to be growing.

Then he heard it.

A low sounding boom, far off in the distance.

He stopped dead in his tracks and waited. After about ten minutes he heard another...

... low sounding boom. It reverberated off the walls then disappeared.

Jack had no idea what it could be but if he didn't know any better he would have guessed it to have been a heartbeat. But that was just too silly.

Wasn't it?

Chapter 31

Hold on

Martha looked all around her. The attic showed no signs of life but her mother's instincts knew better. Her son was near, she was sure of it. In a darkened corner sat a huge mound of straw piled high almost reaching the slanted eaves of the roof. She hoped she would find him there but as she approached a chill shot down her spine, a sensation she had never experienced before and she could smell burnt seaweed. Never had she smelled such a foul odour and she began to wretch. It was coming from within the straw stack. Panic struck her and she lost all fear, something was wrong with her boy, she could sense it. She threw herself on to the loose mound and frantically pulled fistfuls of straw. It cut into her hands but that did not stop her. Then she saw it, a shirt tail. She scrambled through the remaining stack and cried at the sight before her.

Jack's body lay still on the bare floorboards. Her heart lifted. She fell down beside him.

"My boy." Martha sobbed into his ear. "I knew you'd be here. You and Edmund used to hide here when you were younger." She picked up his head, placed it gently on her lap and instantly noticed that he was burning up.

Jack's body was wracked with a fever and under his closed eyelids, his eyes darted savagely from one corner of their sockets to the other.

"Come home to me Jack," Martha implored.

Martha knew dark forces were at work. She wished she had listened to Nanna Tess more attentively when she told her wild tales of her adventures as a child. There was no way Martha could have known the stories Tess told were true. She had admired Tess in so many ways she forgave her the wild fantasies. Tess had raised her grandson Matthew single handily after her son and his wife had died. With her husband already dead Tess raised Matthew as if he were her own son. She knew the sacrifices she had made to feed and clothe him. Tess had welcomed her into her family and she recalled her wedding day. That day Tess had made all the wild flower bouquets and cooked the most sumptuous of meals. The lady had been a tower of strength when she lost her eldest boy Edmund and she helped Jack grow in confidence every day. She could never repay such a debt. Now all Martha wanted was Nanna Tess for guidance. She had never felt so alone in her entire life.

All Martha could do was watch as the life force drained from Jack. Would she lose her whole family in so many days? The thought filled her with horror and she squeezed Jack closer to her.

Jack lay limp in her grasp. As she brought him near she felt something digging into her. She shifted her position and then she saw it, the glowing Talisman on the back of Jack's neck. What should she do? Her immediate instinct was overwhelming. She would remove it. But she paused. This thing could be causing her son's demise but what if it was the one thing keeping him alive. What should she do?

Martha shifted Jack closer to her and she noticed something poking out of his trouser pocket, a piece of paper. She reached down and lifted it out. In her hands, she held the page copied from the Book of the Elderfolk. She saw the sketch in the margin of a man wearing the same Talisman and the one lying on the ground with skull and crossbones over his head, clearly indicating he was dead. She recognised the fact that the Talisman could only be worn in one way. Then she noticed small creatures, she hadn't noticed them at first, they were set into the paper, like a watermark. She held the paper up into the air and she saw wondrous images of all kinds of creatures, none of this world. They almost looked like something that could have stepped out of the stories Tess told Jack when he was a very young child.

Something instinctively told her not to remove the necklace. Instead, she burrowed herself deeper into the straw and hid with her son. She knew all too well she had to think of something and time was fast running out. Doolen would be here for him soon and she had to have a plan.

Would nothing stop the Old Hag? She was certainly not of this earth. Her strength had been remarkable but being able to change from a human into a swarm of insects was against nature. How could a frail woman such as Martha stop her? The Old Hag Doolen could kill her instantly then what would happen to her son? There was no way she was about to let that happen. There had to be a way to stop the horrid Hag and hiding here waiting for certain death wasn't going to save her son.

Chapter 32

Which way?

Jack walked through the new tunnels until he came to a crossroads. He decided to take the higher road. After passing through a winding, weaving tube like structure, he came to a cavern with a huge lake in the centre. It bubbled at the edges. He instantly remembered the lake under the Cloc Mor stone, but that is where the similarity ended. This lake was bubbling for a reason. He had experienced something like that too when his shoe melted in the Red Bog. The lake was one ginormous acid bath and the sticks at the edges washed up on the shore were not sticks, but the bones of a million creatures. There was no way ahead. He had to retreat.

Jack went back to the crossroads. He looked more carefully this time and could have sworn that the edges of these entrances looked almost like muscles. He immediately dismissed the idea and knew he had no choice but to take the lower road. He did not know what exactly he was searching for; he only hoped he would know when he found it.

The new pathway led on for an age until he came to the edge of what looked like a giant forest. He couldn't be quite sure for even with his newfound vision, it was darker here, harder to make things out. Strange sounds, like air rushing overhead and around his feet, unsettled him and he could not explain where the breeze was coming from.

He carried on and as he went he studied the trees more closely. To his surprise he realised they were not trees at all, just structures that he associated with trees. What were they? He reached out a claw and touched the trunk of one. His hand stuck fast, glued to the surface by some thick jelly. He placed his other claw around his wrist and yanked hard. Luckily after the third attempt he broke free. This was not a forest at all. It was a deadly place, worse, nearly than the lake of acid.

The only thing that kept Jack sane was the knowledge that if things did get too serious he could jump back into his own body but he also knew that would be the last chance he would ever have of climbing back into the Shimnavore's body if he abandoned it now. He would be letting his father down and he would never let that happen. He trudged on knowing that soon he would find what he sought.

The ground under his feet grew warmer as he moved forward. He knew there must be a heat source up ahead and with it maybe some proper light. He could open his eyes again and see properly.

Then it happened.

The whole forest shook violently and the boom Jack had heard earlier resounded all around him. He fell to his knees and held onto the first thing he could grab as a gale blew over his back. As quick as it came it stopped. Jack knew he might not last the next wave of whatever it was. He got up and ploughed on. To his left he noticed one of the larger trees had a huge gash running through it- a great big cut in the tree. He decided to take a chance and look inside. It was against his better judgement but for some reason it felt like the right thing to do. His head was telling him to do one thing but his heart told him another. His head lost the argument.

Inside the tree ran long pipes and they all headed in one direction. He crawled along one of them on his claws and knees and just up ahead he could see light. He opened his eyes.

Yes, it was light- a beautiful white light. Now he could not tear his gaze away from it. He crawled onward. At the end of the pipe he came to a ledge and looked down. There was a large chamber below. It was too big a drop and the pathway down looked treacherous. He decided to rest for a moment but after ten minutes the ground shook all about him, as if it were in spasm. He could feel his clawed feet begin to be crushed within the fibres of some strange undergrowth.

Then ...

...BOOM.

A massive convulsive force threw Jack right into the heart of the chamber and he braced for impact as he fell. But to his astonishment his landing was softer than he could have imagined. That is when it dawned on him. He wasn't in the heart of the chamber... more precisely he was in the chamber of a heart. He was in a heart... a living heart.

A hundred images flashed through his mind. The tunnel entrance he had come through had not been lined with stalagmites and stalactites as he first thought. They were definitely not carved either. They were teeth and the soft pathways he had just walked over were not pathways at all but arteries and veins, the lake was the acid-filled stomach and the sticky forest were the lungs.

Then it hit him. He knew where he was. The Dullahan had warned him. Jack realised he was in the very heart of an enormous creature...

...The All-Seer

Chapter 33

In the Forest

From within the deep lungs of the All-Seer many eyes opened for the first time in centuries. They stretched their sinewy arms and muscular legs and then finally their telescopic necks.

The Shimnavore awoke.

They knew instantly that the last Shimnavore must have entered the mouth of the All-Seer because the spell that kept their race in a deep sleep had been broken. Ever since they had breached the Silver Orb and crossed the Mourne Wall they were cursed to walk the Devil's Coachroad and into the jaws of the All-Seer.

But why had this Shimnavore not joined them? They had to find out.

Where had it gone?

Hordes of Shimnavore stood in row upon row as far as the eye could see. Their stench grew thick as they gathered and together they set forth from the lung-forest to search through the body of the All-Seer. Not one of them had noticed the gash in the tree but it wouldn't be long before they did.

Roars, grunts and a half-attempt at speech let the Shimnavore communicate with one another. They were a primitive race with only one goal. To rule. They had no drive or ambition, they did not strive for a better world, and they only saw the beauty in the demise of every other race. They wanted supremacy over everything and they needed the last piece of the jigsaw.

The All-Seer had no blood in its veins or arteries. For so long had it been locked under the mountain it was without such life-force. The humongous beast would have to be wakened before the blood would flow again and luckily for Jack because he would have long since drowned in the heart of the megalithic creature.

Instead Jack just sat in awe staring up at a shard of glass filled with light and darkness. It penetrated the heart and looked like a mortal wound. It was quite possible that this is what caused the gash in the tree-like structure he had just come through. But what was this giant splinter of glass that could have brought down the All-Seer? Jack rose to his clawed feet and approached the shiny object. The room around him glowed red from the light reflected off the object. Jack could see the musculature of the All-Seer's heart. The chamber he stood in must have been the size of the harbour in Annalong. He found it impossible to imagine the actual size of the creature but he knew one thing. He did not want to wake it.

Jack drew nearer to the shard and a chilled feeling began to run down his long curved spine just like his first ever sighting of the Shimnavore way back when he stood in his garden in the snow. But this chill would not leave him. As if thousands of icy cold fingers were running up and down his back. He elongated his telescopic neck and his eyes were only a few inches from the glassy walls. The piece he stared into remained dark and he found it difficult to focus but suddenly a flash of bright light shot out towards him. Startled, he stumbled backwards a few steps. He approached a second time, more cautious and aware of what might happen. He looked into the dark section again and waited to see the light.

Yes…

A flicker of light. Jack could make out a shape.

A face… It vanished instantly but Jack convinced himself he knew who it was. He decided to try the sight he had used when he walked the dark corridors and he closed his eyes. The glass shard took on a whole new life. In the tinged green light Jack could make out everything more clearly. They were all faces, faces of the Ancients, the Elderfolk and something else. Something not of either race but familiar to both. He followed its energy until it seemed to settle for a moment. Jacks heart would have skipped a beat had he a beating heart in his chest but the excitement he felt was still real. The flicker of light had a form and that form was his father. Matthew's soul was trapped with all the others.

Then Jack noticed something else, something on the other side of the glass shard. A face looking in from the outside just like him with two dark pearl eyes set inside a withered skull…

…The Old Hag Doolen.

But how could this be possible? Jack quickly ran round to the side of the shard looking for her but there were no signs of life. She wasn't in the room with him but somehow she could see what he could see.

Jack could hear shouts from beyond the heart's chamber as marauding hordes of Shimnavore scoured the All-Seers body. Their anger grew with each passing moment. They had been locked away for so long, forced to sleep forever but the last of their kind had resurrected them but he was nowhere to be found. Where was the last Shimnavore?

Jack tried to understand everything before him. Doolen had definitely been looking into the shard just like him. What if she were looking in from the Outer Realm? But how could she have such power? He thought hard and then it came to him. She must have her hands on the pages of the Elderfolk that Tess transcribed. He remembered what he saw on them; the Tree in the Tree, the Talisman, but he had that in his pocket and pages of the Shimnvore dancing around a dragon-like being.

No wait. He assumed the dragon-like creature in the centre of the circle to be the All-Seer but the more he remembered the picture the more he realised and the clearer it became. The Shimnavore were dancing in a giant circle all right but it wasn't around the All-Seer. They were dancing around one gigantic sleeping Shimnavore

Was that why they were searching for him? Did they need him to wake it?

Jack knew he hadn't much time before they found him and either forced him to join them or just kill him. He went back to the shard of glass and looked at it from top to bottom. He had been right, the shard looked as though it had pierced the heart of the All-Seer and killed it. What worried him is what would happen if such an object were destroyed. Would removing it allow the heart to heal and give life back to the All-Seer. Then what would happen. The size of the creature along could destroy whole villages with a single swipe.

He decided to put such thoughts to the back of his mind. He had only one reason to be there and it was within his grasp. He reached out a talon and scraped it along the glass. Instantly the shapes inside flocked around his claw. Jack had his eyes closed and he could make out their shapes easily. Then one form came to the front...

...His father.

Without hesitation, Jack plunged his hand forward and a blazing pain shot through his arm as if it had been immersed in acid.

It burned so badly, so painfully.

Chapter 34

The Attic

Martha clung to her son and willed him to hang on. She thought for a moment about Matthew and questioned what she might have done wrong to bring about such a tragedy. But she didn't let the thought linger too long. Nanna Tess had taught her better.

But in amongst the straw, that covered them both, Martha could still see. Enough light penetrated to let her make out her son's ghostly white body. She watched every rise and fall of his chest grateful he was still breathing. He lay flaccid in her arms until suddenly his hand began to twitch, the first movement he had made since she had found him. To her horror, large blisters rose up on the back of his hand and spread along his forearm and she could see from his grimaced face that he was in tremendous pain.

She knew she had her son in her arms but like Matthew, Jack's mind was elsewhere; a world away.

"Hang on Jack. I don't know where you are but I know you're out there trying to save your father. I'm here keeping you safe, but hurry back son, you need to hurry back."

Then the smell hit Martha's nostrils. The putrid smell of something like burnt seaweed and it came from the fresh wound on Jack's arm. She tore a strip of cloth from her dress and wrapped around his burnt flesh. A part of her knew that the odour might attract the Old Hag.

She still had no plans how to defend them if Doolen did find them. Martha clenched her fist and she realised she had Tess' copy of the page from the Elderfolk's book in her grasp. She had reached for it unknowingly. But how could it help? She looked at it again and realised she had forgotten to do something so obvious. She had been so enthralled with the page of the creatures on the page that she never thought what might be written on the other side.

She turned the page and her hand began to shake. She stared at the image in the centre and slowly she realised what she had to do, what any mother would do. It might be her last act but for her son she gladly accepted the fact.

Martha crouched in closer to Jack and she waited for the Old Hag. She was ready for her.

Chapter 35

Cracked

Jack's enormous yellowed teeth bit into his blood red gums and he let out an anguished howl. His skin bubbled and blistered but he held his arm out straight, unfaltering, in the hope he would find his father's soul or that it might just find its way to him. Would he recognise that the Shimnavore's body he inhabited was actually his own son? Jack waited for what seemed like an eternity and then he knew he only had one option left.

The Shimnavore's head twisted around so its eyes were pointing back into the chamber of the heart. Then its neck extended at lightning speed and its muzzle penetrated the glass shard as well. Any lesser being would have died instantly but luckily the Shimnavore was already dead. Pain washed over it like oceans of acid but still he carried on. He roared out into the vast emptiness...

...DAAAA.

He could stand the pain no longer and he began to withdraw his face. Little did he think about the consequences of his actions on his own frail body back in the attic of the Old Mill.

But still he left his arm inside the glass wall and waited and endured the suffering. Then something quite miraculous happened. Something touched his clawed hand. Jack wrapped his hand around the object and held on tight. It was another hand, dwarfed in his own. Then he felt it, a familiar bump in the palm. He held it tighter and with a mighty tug he pulled the soul from its prison.

An ethereal light lit up the heart's chamber. Jack stood staring in wonderment at the sight. The body of the Shimnavore dwarfed the outline but it was unquestionably the image of his beloved father. Jack felt his heart skip a beat. He didn't care how impossible that might sound but it was as if a lightning bolt had struck him and charged him with a new energy. He reached out a talon and hoped his father would not be afraid of a Shimnavore's opened claw.

But far from being afraid, Matthew extended his own hand and reached up and stroked the hair that surrounded his son's eyes. He could see the tears pouring from them and he glowed even more intensely.

A voice as soft as a whisper came from his lips, "Don't cry Jack, my beautiful son, my hero. There is still more to be done."

And with that Matthew's image began to fade and shrink until it became no bigger than a pebble. With clumsy talons, Jack picked up the tiny object. It looked just like the diamond on a Talisman. In his brutish claw, he held his father's soul. Now he needed to return it to its rightful owner.

A sudden snarling cry echoed across the chamber but it did not come from Jack. He instinctively looked up to the direction of the sound and there standing on the ledge, were two Shimnavore. They had found him. What should he do? His first instinct was to run but he wondered how far he would get. He could see another way out of the chamber but where it might lead, he had no idea. He knew they would be faster than he was for he was still growing accustomed to the disjointed manner in which he moved. And if they caught sight of his eyes the game would surely be up. He decided to follow them.

To his surprise, as soon as he approached them they turned their fronts on him and walked away. Never for an instant had they suspected anything. Jack let out a huge sigh of relief. Where were they taking him, he had no idea but at the first chance, he would make a run for it. All he needed to do was pick the right moment. He squeezed the tiny jewel in his hand and began to climb out of the chamber. He took one glance back at the huge glass shard and just before he climbed through the tunnel he swore he saw a crack in the flawless glass.

Jack kept his eyes closed the whole time so he could see clearly and the pain in his muzzle distracted him a little from what he was about to witness. After a long and difficult walk, Jack's two guides stopped and grunted at him. They pointed forward and walked ahead of him. Jack could not move. He was transfixed, for below him in a giant valley were hundreds of dancing Shimnavore. Dancing in ever larger concentric circles like ripples on a lake.

A creeping dread overwhelmed Jack and he took a small step backward for in the centre of the circles something was emerging- something huge. Something was waking up.

Just as Jack thought things couldn't get any worse, to his horror, an enormous Shimnavore rose out of the hordes. Jack could see something moving under the leathery skin of the creature's back. It flexed its gargantuan muscles and two bones twice the size of tall ships' masts burst out and shot into the air with sails as dark as death lashing out like they were caught in a storm. They unfurled and cascaded down the Giant Shimnavore's back.

They were colossal wings.

The Mighty Shimnavore turned around. Two molten-red eyes stared out from the back of its head right at Jack. They seemed to pierce him and know instantly of his treachery. Jack took another step backward but he stumbled. The cavernous mouth of the newly awoken beast opened, volcanic flames erupted from between sharpened teeth, and it bellowed, "Bring me the impostor."

The voice sounded like coarse gravel and Jack's bones reverberated inside the shell of his body. "Bring him to me, dead or alive."

Jack turned and began to run but one of the Shimnavore was too fast for him. It pounced on him and bit into his neck. The pain tore deep but he dodged sideways and the bite didn't penetrate as deeply as it could have. Jack summoned up the last of his strength and jerked his neck with all his might. The teeth loosened their hold for an instant and he managed to slip free.

"You cannot escape me."

Jack raced on, closely pursued by the handful of Shimnavore that had yet to join the dancing hordes. He wouldn't let himself believe there was no way out. He knew that upward would lead back to the mouth he had so willingly entered before. His claws gripped the fleshy ground of the All-Seer's throat as Jack made his escape but the other Shimnavore were catching up on him. He caught a fleeting glimpse of them as he rounded a corner, heading ever upwards. Their eyes glowed like torches as they closed in on him.

It couldn't be far, it just couldn't. They were bearing down on him as he spied the stalagmite and stalactite teeth of the All-Seer. He sped up and was running across the thick spongy entranceway that he now knew to be a tongue. He only had a short distance. A claw lashed out at him from behind and caught the tendon near his ankle and it tore through it. Jack ignored the pain for he could see the opening just ahead. He sprang forward toward the gaping hole and closed his eyes. He knew he had to make it but a pain coursed through his body as he bounced off the empty space. The membrane covering the exit to the All-Seer's mouth was made out of the same substance as the Silver Orb.

He had only seconds to live. The other Shimnavore licked their lips and thick slobbers of saliva dripped from their muzzles as they gathered around him. They would take great delight ripping him to shreds. It did not matter to them if he was brought back dead. Jack only cared for one thing, well two things really. He knew if he died where he stood then his own body would die back in his own realm but that thought did not matter as much as his father's soul would be trapped in this stinking place for all eternity.

Then it struck him. He had the answer in his grasp.

Jack opened his claw and the tiny diamond shone brightly from within the folds of his skin. It did not fall for Jack had it clenched in his grip...

...His father's soul.

The other Shimnavore pounced on him. As they were in mid air Jack turned and slashed his open claw against the Orb-Like membrane and the diamond soul tore through it like a sword though a veil. He dived out through the hole and fell out onto the steps beyond.

In a single reflex action he twisted his neck and watched in delight as the other Shimnavore bounced off the wall of energy that had instantly sealed up. They landed back on the ground but they didn't give up. They leapt against the entrance again and hammered at the membrane stopping their release. They were trapped and Jack knew that now they were awake they were destined to be eternally hungry. But the All-Seer's body surrounded them so they could feast for quite some time before their real hunger would start.

His delight was short lived because from deep within the heart of the All-Seer a wail burst forth. It echoed along the arteries and through the miles of veins until it reached the mouth of the slumbering beast and not even the Orb-like membrane dampened its ferocity. The tunnel walls encompassing Jack began to shake from the Giant Shimnavore's cries. Then without warning, the rocks overhead started to dislodge and began to fall.

Jack got back onto his feet as quickly as he could and he began to make his way back up through the tunnels he had descended earlier. However, this time the walls were collapsing in around him, trying to ensure that his final resting place would be in the core of the mountain. Jack limped onward, the pain in his leg throbbing slowing his progress but the feeling of warmth in his hand gave him the comfort he so desperately needed. Just knowing that his father was close was enough to make him strong. He could almost hear his voice in his mind willing him on and it gave him hope.

The crumbling rocks soon became boulders and they fell at an ever increasing speed. The screams coming from behind Jack did not let up. The King Shimnavore knew his fate was sealed and he would do everything in his power to bring Jack Turner down with him.

Jack's clawed talons on his Shimnavore body gripped and released the stone steps at lightning speed. The pain from his injury he tried to bury deep in his mind. He could not let the damage to his body slow him down. All he could hear now was his father's voice and he focused on it. It drowned out the deafening rumble of the mountain caving in all around him. Then suddenly, up ahead a sight to make a Shimnavore's heart lift...

...LIGHT... MOONLIGHT.

Jack sped up. Now the rocks were falling in front of him trying to block the entrance to the tunnel but he did not slow down. He kept on, for his goal was now in plain sight. His father's soul had to be set free.

Jack tumbled out of the entrance just as a giant slab of rock fell against it, sealing the tunnel for good. He fell from the ledge and bounced down the side of the cliff until landing heavily on his side. The sound of several ribs cracking filled his ears. The Shimnavore's lifespan was coming to an end. He hadn't long left but he still had a ways to go.

He was now back on the Devil's Coachroad. He clenched his fist as tight as he could and buried the tiny diamond deep into the scaly folds of his skin to try and drown out any sign of his father's energy emitted from his soul. He raced down the granite scree as fast as his Shimnavore's legs would carry him. The Coachroad joined in with the mountains outrage and it too began to close in on him. The walls of granite tightened as he stumbled onward but Jack would never let it win. He had a life to save and a father to bring home. He had a mother who needed her husband. He had hope in the palm of his hand and the mountain would never take that away from him.

Then he spied them in the distance, standing like the loyal companions he knew them to be. He knew now that no matter what was thrown at him he wouldn't be beaten for standing on the threshold of the Devil's Coachroad were Cobs, the Dullahan and Trom.

Cobs and the Dullahan felt the huge rumblings of the hillside before they saw Jack. They ran to the brink of the pathway and waved frantically and yelled as loudly as they could when they saw Jack falling, rolling over grey shale, picking himself back up, and sprinting onward. The hulking disjointed frame almost looked elegant in the final steps as Jack crashed through the end of the Coachroad. He came to rest right at their feet and his eyes beamed victory at them. He opened his talons and relaxed his clawed grip around the precious jewel he held.

The tiny diamond of light shone brightly in his scaly palm. The Dullahan, Cobs and Trom looked on in wonder at the dazzling vision in front of them. A human soul was the most wondrous treasure any of them had ever had the privilege to see. The light grew brighter until none of them could bear to gaze upon it any longer. Even Jack was forced to close his eyes. But when he did he could see again with the same sight he had in the tunnels of the mountain. He saw the outline of his father again only this time he was grinning like he did when he'd had a great catch of fish. Jack knew that his father was about to do something extraordinary.

The outline of his father morphed into a bird of pure white flame and it lifted into the sky and rode majestically on the warm air currents. It flew higher and higher, further and further until Jack could only see a tiny speck of light that finally merged with all the other stars.

Matthew was going home. Everyone opened their eyes again and looked at Jack.

"You did it Jack, you did it," shouted Cobs who danced a jig at the Feet of the Dullahan.

"I never doubted you for a second," said the Dullahan and he placed a hand on Jack's shoulder. At that very moment he wouldn't have cared if touching the Shimnavore aged him one hundred years.

"To tell you the truth Jack, I'm glad you're back and all but I'm even happier that I'm in my own skin," said Trom.

To say the Shimnavore laughed is a hard thing to prove but the sound that came from Jack's muzzle sounded as close to a laugh as ever a Shimnavore could hope to make. The four companions stood and watched the last of the Devil's Coachroad fall and they decided a feast was called for. The celebrations would still be underway at the Curraghard Tree for the shattering of the Silver Orb but wait until they heard about this latest escapade. Jack would be held in even higher esteem.

The sight of a hulking great Shimnavore, a headless man and two tiny Clurichauns heading up Rocky Mountain and heading for home is a rare occurrence, one that needs to be treasured. A more unlikely bunch of friends would never roam the Mournes again. They quickly climbed Slieve Donard, stood at the tower on its peak, and surveyed all the Mournes beneath them.

"There is no better place in all the lands," said Trom.

"I agree. It truly is a place apart," replied Cobs

From their vantage point they could see the small fires right across the hills, down in the valleys and in Tollymore Forest where they were headed. The lands were rejoicing the collapse of the Silver Orb.

New and better times were coming.

The feeling of belonging in the Shimnavore's husk was becoming almost too hard to resist. With this body Jack could conquer the world. He could have creatures at his beck and call. He could crush anyone underfoot, he could tear anyone limb for limb. The thoughts of domination were coming faster now, faster, stronger....harder to resist. The urge to kill...

"Noooooooo," the Shimnavore roared. Its sinewy muscles were taught and in spasm. Jack threw himself on to the ground and writhed in agony. Cobs was quickly at his side.

"Time's run out Jack," said Cobs. "You have to leave this body now or you'll be trapped in it forever. Now concentrate. Think of your body back home."

Jack tried to concentrate but the thoughts and feelings of the Shimnavore overwhelmed him.

"Close your eyes Jack and think of being with your father. Do not open them whatever you do. You need to focus. Do not let the Shimnavore win."

Jack closed his eyes but terrible images of all that the Shimnavore had done whilst it lived flashed through his mind. He witnessed the Holocene, he saw his great-aunt Grace and all the Hawksbeards being chased over the hills, he saw small creatures being stamped on and eaten...He could bear it no longer and he opened his eyes. The second he did he instantly lost his place, his time and now something worse began to happen; a million voices began whispering into his ears. They kept repeating the same thing over and over again incessantly, getting louder and louder until they were all roaring in unison...

No up, no down,

No time to flow,

No heat, no noise,

Nowhere to go,

Forever and ever

And ever remain,

Until at last,

You're driven insane.

Jack had lost all sense of time listening to the voices. He had no idea how long he had been there; a day, a week, a month, an eternity. He only hoped it had been seconds for he knew his father had not much time left. He had to get home and nothing was going to stop him. He had to believe his mind had just played a trick on him. With all his willpower, Jack forced his eyes shut again.

The voices disappeared instantly.

The Shimnavore was dead.

Chapter 36

Trapped

The Old Hag Doolen stepped back from her cauldron and threw both her arms high into the air. She screamed an incomprehensible incantation to the four winds. Her deathly pale skin suddenly darkened and her flesh began to stir as she turned from flesh and bones into a shadow of horror. Every candle on the walls flickered madly then snuffed out in an instant.

The Old Hag transformed into the insect swarm of pitch-black darkness, a nightmare brought to life with a hellish hunger that would only be satisfied by the body of Jack Turner.

The insect cloud lifted high into the air and flew up the stone steps out of the crypt and into the night sky. Every bat and last minute swallow flew as fast as their wings would beat to escape the pathway of the Hag's destruction. The ones that didn't move fast enough were devoured whole. Only their skeletal remains falling to the earth let anyone know of their existence.

Nothing would stop this evil being from reaching its destination and wreaking havoc once she did.

Martha grasped Jack tighter to her chest. It had been horrific to see his arms blistering but when the skin on his face began to burn she could not contain her anger. She could not have known that at that precise moment Jack's arm and muzzle had entered the glass shard as the Shimnavore. Whatever happened to the Shimnavore's body in the InBetween affected Jack in the Outer Realm. She shouted out, blaming everything for what was happening to her son but deep down she was so grateful that he was still alive. She had to check his eyes. Had they been burned too? She gently lifted his eyelids to check on them and got the fright of her life when the two deathly monstrous eyes of a Shimnavore stared back at her. Martha almost let Jack's head drop the shock was so overwhelming. They were not the eyes of her son. She screamed. What had happened to her precious son? She had to hold on, be strong for him. She knew he would come back to her and that thought kept her sane.

But now the stench of burnt seaweed from Jack's wounds grew more noxious. It would draw the Old Hag Doolen to him like bees to honey.

Martha knew she hadn't long to save her son but she was ready. Her task would be simple. It was clearly drawn on Tess' page of the Elderfolk. One day she hoped Jack would understand what she was about to do. Being a parent is the single most important job in the entire world and many would tell you their love would move heaven and earth to make their sick child well. Martha Turner was one such mother.

The storm clouds grew thicker over the Old Mill and it lit up every time a streak of lightning pierced the air. The smell of ozone filled the air.

From the graveyard the dark cloud came. It moved at an alarming rate until it reached the mill. It swirled around and around, faster with each turn until a raging tornado of insects spun uncontrollably toward the wooden doors. The enormous plague pressed heavily against them and the large wooden beam Martha had lodged on the other side strained.

The swarm pressed again and this time the wooden beam bowed.

Again the swarm pressed and the beam cracked.

One more thrust and the wooden beam shattered into a million fragments. The door of the mill burst open and at its threshold stood the shadowy form of an old woman in a cloud of darkness.

Martha held her breath and grabbed Jack closer to her. She kissed him on the forehead and set him back onto the bare floorboards. She whispered into his ear, "goodbye my love."

Martha crawled out from her hiding place and stood up. She walked close to the attic ledge and looked down below her.

The Old Hag stared back up at her, the veins in her forehead clearly visible even from that distance. A bony finger pointed up at Martha and it beckoned her to come down. The Old Hag broke her gaze and looked down at the broken ladder and cackled. She had them trapped; they had no way of escape.

Chapter 37

Old Mill

Martha took a step back from the ledge. She had seen the ladder broken on the ground next to the Old Hag and sighed with relief for another ladder sat in the straw where Jack hid. Doolen couldn't get up this high Martha convinced herself.

This would buy her some time. Martha looked at the page in her hand once again. A cloud of darkness locked in battle with a cloud of light. If the cloud of light was supposed to be her would she have to die to free her spirit to fight this evil entity? But when the time had come, she could not jump to her death. What if she was wrong? Who would defend Jack?

As Martha stood staring at the picture trying to make sense of it she didn't notice Doolen. The half-transformed Hag rose up over the edge of the attic floor and hovered over her head. The bottom half of her wicked form swarmed about in a blur of scuttling insects. She flew from side to side, her robes thrashing about like giant bat wings.

She hissed at Martha, "give me the boy and I'll make sure you don't suffer," she shifted in the air once again, "for too long." Doolen cackled uncontrollably. She knew Jack's hiding place and could see the dim white glow from the Talisman. But before she took what she thought rightly to be hers she would have her revenge.

Martha felt a prickling sensation course through her body and she recognised it as anger mixed with defeat. She was at the mercy of the creature in front of her. Doolen swept in and swiped at Martha cutting her cheek. A small trickle of blood ran down the side of her face. Instinctively she put her hand to it then looked at her bloodstained fingers.

"Is that all you've got you rotten excuse for a corpse," Martha goaded.

"Oh. I'm only starting my dear." The Old hag threw her head back and the laugh that spurted forth from her throat turned Martha's hair white.

It was Martha's turn to laugh. "Thank you, you wizened pile of bugs. I always liked Tess' white hair, now I've just the same."

This only enraged Doolen.

"Tess cursed me to live in that tomb but her death freed me and I could travel again into the night."

"Travel," laughed Martha. "You look like you prefer cockroach to stagecoach."

"You try my patience woman." Doolen rushed to Martha and swatted her like someone annoyed with a fly. Martha flew though the air and landed next to Jack. Luckily, the straw dampened her fall. She was dazed but far from unconscious. Doolen reached in past her and grabbed Jack by the scruff of his neck. The Talisman glowed brightly on the back of his neck and she grinned, staring at its beauty. It had been so long since she had felt its glow.

"Come to me." Doolen spoke directly to the Talisman almost as if it could understand her. She held Jack's limp body over the ledge and she spoke straight into his unconscious face. "I have one more need for you boy. I'll get my Talisman off you in just a moment. I know we will both perish if I try to take it off you whilst you're still alive. And if I kill you it will tarnish both halves of the Talisman. But if you were to die as the result of an accident my dear one."

The Hag opened her hand.

Martha screamed as she watched in horror as her son fell to his death.

Chapter 38

Fighting Spirit

Martha threw out her arm towards her son in desperation but it was too late, his limp body disappeared over the ledge. Doolen flew over Martha's head and from within her shadow of horror five black jagged fingers emerged and sharp yellowed nails slashed ferociously at her back. Martha's dress became a tatter of ribbons within seconds.

The Old Hag lashed again and again. Martha knew she couldn't take much more of the torment she was being put through. She lay drenched in sweat, her eyes sunk deep inside her sockets. She did not look long for the world.

But the sight before her gave her a renewed strength. She thought that for a moment it was an apparition.

Over the edge of the attic arose a white cloud-like mist. In its centre was Jack.

Jack's eyes flew wide open and he stared straight at his mother.

"We have come to save you Ma."

Martha looked confused. She had no idea how what she was witnessing was possible. But she didn't care. The sight of her son alive was enough for her to hold on.

The Old Hag spat and hissed. She swirled up into a cascade of stench-filled terror and soared up even higher into the peak of the Old Mill.

Jack had never hit the bottom. Matthew's soul was returning from the InBetween and sensed the danger his son was in. It knew where to find him and rather than return to his own body he knew he could do more in the form he had become...Pure energy. Pure love.

The cloud of white hovered over Martha and placed Jack by her side. She could see the burns on his face were gone. Somehow Matthew had healed him.

"Here Ma. Quick," shouted Jack. He pulled the Talisman chains over his head and broke the Talisman in two. "Put this on."

Jack could see Martha was terrified. She was unable to move. He didn't hesitate for a second to come to his mother's aid. He lifted the chain and placed it over her head. The Talisman glowed around her neck. The other Talisman around Jack's neck burned just as brightly. They were now soul mates. Martha could feel everything her son experienced and he could sense her pain. But they both shared something much more powerful; their love for each other and their love for Matthew. Jack smiled at his mother and she returned the gesture.

Matthew's energy enveloped Martha and she could hear him in her thoughts. She could see all their shared memories and see their son Edmund smiling back at them both. If she died at this very moment, she would die happy but that was not to be. The white mist lifted from around Martha and rose up into the air. Her pain lifted from her too and she noticed that no more blood flowed from her wounds. She had no more wounds- they had healed miraculously. Even the dress on her back had been mended.

With their minds and souls united they knew they had unimaginable strength but to take on the Hag was terrifying. This creature had a dark magic at her command. How could they defeat such a demon?

The white foggy mist of Matthew's energy churned. It moved towards Jack and rolled around him but never once did it darken. It rose and fell in tumultuous folds of light and air as if an invisible hand of a conductor was orchestrating its movements. Fold upon fold of clear spray turned in upon itself until it began to thicken, whipped up in the frenzy with Jack at the core feeding off the energy from Matthew's soul. Jack lifted off the ground.

The dark mist of hatred that was Doolen and bright mist of the Turner men lifted high up into the mill, hovering across from one another. Off in the distance the bells of the boats in the harbour rang out.

A death knell?

The clouds of light and darkness began to stretch and distort. Then, without warning Jack and Martha shouted in unison.

"Now."

The two formations rushed towards each other and they collided in an explosion of thunderous anger. A storm of wills, a battle of light and darkness. The Old Hag Doolen's evil spirit locked horns with that of the good-

224

natured Jack. Except for one thing, Jack may have been pure of heart but he certainly was no longer good-natured. He would stop at nothing to rid the world of anything that would bring harm to his family.

Every now and then from within the dark and light clouds a feature would rise up and take shape; a random feature of the Hag, perhaps a bony cheek or the contour of her pointed chin. Then the warty outline of the crooked beak upon the Doolen's horrid face.

The white light soared up as if on the wings of a lark and began to envelop the darkness but Doolen was too quick. She dived towards Martha, who stood on the attic floor, and a hand came out from the cloud, grabbed her by the throat, and lifted her off her feet. Martha choked in the vice like grip and her eyes grew sunken. They seemed to be falling into their sockets. Her life force was being drained, feeding the Old Hag's cloud-like form. She was growing in strength as Martha weakened. Death soaked the cloud but Jack would not stand by and watch his mother die.

Just as a cloud forms by tiny droplets of water so too was the Turner's cloud of light. Except their tiny droplets were memories, good times and bad times spent as a family. They are what formed Jack and made him who he was. Even the tragedies in his life helped make him the man he had become. The milk-white mist devoured the darkness and Martha dropped back onto the attic floor. But the darkness fought back with every grain of evil she could muster. She remembered what she wished for most, to rule over the InBetween but now that was not enough. She wanted absolute power over everything and the Talisman would bring that about. No weak spirit would stop that.

Shards of darkness penetrated the light and it began to dissolve. Thunder roared as they collided. It was to be the final battle of darkness and light and it looked as though Jack would not be the victor.

Martha lay on the attic floor watching her son do battle with the most evil force in the world.

She put her hand to her crushed throat and ignored the excruciating pain when she shouted to her Jack.

"Do it for Matthew. Do it for your Da."

Martha knew Jack heard her, for even though she thought all hope was lost and the dark cloud that encompassed Jack and had almost extinguished his light she saw a faint flicker. Then something more. A bolt of lightning streaked across the dark storm cloud illuminating them from within and Martha heard a scream of pain. The Old Hag had been wounded.

"Again Jack, use whatever strength Matthew is giving you. You've got her on the run."

The encouragement worked again for a second thunderbolt tore through the blackness. Martha could make out a bird-like form emerging from the insect swarm of black- a phoenix rising from the ashes of despair. Jack had used every part of his being, his love of his family, his need to see them again, to be with them. An explosion of light engulfed the dark cloud. Jack's love was pure. Flames of white leapt through the sinister murkiness and every part of it burned. The vile creature cried out,

"Help me, I'm becoming nothing." A final scream filled the room and the swarm of insects dropped to the floor of the Old Mill. They scuttled over to the shadows. Slaters, slugs and silverfish writhing over one another just as they had done over Jack's boots when he first come across the Old Hag the night he unlocked the secret door to the True Kingdom of Mourne.

Jack fell to the floor exhausted and Martha held her son in her arms. They knew the Hag had just lost the most important battle of all, she had lost the war; one that they, the Turner's, had won.

Matthew had fought valiantly too but now it was time to return to his body. To be reunited with his physical self. The cloud of light lifted up into the air once more and slowly drifted out the huge Mill doors and off into the darkness like a white knight.

Chapter 39

Reunion

Matthew's dying body still lay in David Burn's house. He had been there since the fire in the cottage. His condition had not improved in the few hours since the Hag's death but neither had it got any worse. He looked colourless as if his life had been drained from him.

Martha and Jack climbed down the ladder from the attic and made their way into the village. They were told where Matthew could be found. But Jack told his mother he would follow her along. He had one more thing to do.

Martha sat on the bed next to Matthew. She squeezed his hand and spoke softly in his ear.

"There is someone who so desperately wants to speak to you Matthew," said Martha.

Still he did not waken.

Amongst the void Matthew had become lost but he could see a glimmer, a flicker in the distance. It was more than a glimmer of hope and more than a memory. Matthew reached out in his mind and clutched at it. He recognised something from his life, something of his very own.

Away in the distance there came a familiar sound…

…a tune.

…Someone was whistling a tune- his tune.

He stirred.

Matthew's eyes flickered for just an instant. Martha lifted his head and turned it up towards her face.

"That's it Matthew. I know you're in there. Come home to me, come home to me."

A faint memory stirred in Matthew but the sound continued to grow stronger and with it his recall.

He focused on the sound. He tried his best to remember it. It was his soul. And it was returning to him. Reuniting and making him whole again.

Matthew's eyes were moving rapidly now and then without warning he opened them. He stared up into the eyes of his wife and smiled.

"We did it," he said. "Can't you hear the tune?"

Martha smiled back at him. "I can hear it."

Matthew hugged his wife for all he was worth. She was his hero. She hugged him back for what seemed like an eternity and after she loosened her grip, he could move. He didn't waste a moment, he leapt to his feet. A new lease of life coursed through him as the tune grew louder. He threw off the quilt and jumped down to the ground. He ran out the door and down the hillside as fast as his feet would carry him towards the pier. The tune grew louder with every passing second.

Matthew came to an abrupt stop, skidding in the gravel underfoot.

Standing on the end of the pier in the golden glow of the Irish sunrise stood Jack happily whistling Fiddler's Green.

Matthew joined him. He towered against the brightening sky.

Jack sprang up into the loving arms of his Da and looked into his eyes. There was no need for words... Jack snuggled in close to Mathew's chest and breathed in the smell of the sea. He was home.

Chapter 40

Time to Pay

The All-Seer stirred.

The End...

...is coming.